THUNDER

Sata

A.G

Prologue

THUNDER

I Don't Date

There's a lot I do for my brothers, but this is a new one for me. Hammer and I must have drawn the short straw, because here we are outside a florist shop picking up pink fucking roses and centerpieces for the elaborate party Priest is throwing, with the help of the Lady Pride, so that he can celebrate his engagement to his woman, Quinn, in style.

I'm happy as hell for him, but I'd rather be doing the liquor run. Priest is going to ask Quinn to marry him, again, at the clubhouse. It seems that once wasn't enough for Priest to hear her say yes, and between Willow and Vi, the place looks more like a gala banquet than a guys' hang-out. He wants his family there to celebrate. We already know Quinn is head over heels in love with Priest and this is just an excuse for all of us to come together. Those two belong together. Priest also arranged to have Quinn's family come out for the affair. For a kid who came from such a messed-up home, Priest finally has the family he deserves.

Hammer and I get out of the club's truck—apparently, we're going to be filling the back with flowers—and walk up to the store called Petals. The place looks like something out of a fairy-tale book. Loads of flowers are expected, but it's filled with twinkle lights and sparkles. I could just see Vi's daughter, Gabby, go apeshit in this place. That little girl is such a girly girl, and if she grows up as pretty as her mother, Orion's going to need to get her a personal bodyguard to hold the boys back.

The bell chimes over the door as we move inside.

"Be right there," a soft voice says from the back room. Something about the voice sounds familiar. Really familiar, eerily so. A moment later, a woman emerges from the back, and it's like a heavy weight lands on my chest, knocking the wind out of me. She's a dark brunette with chocolate-brown eyes, olive skin, and a body that any man would walk through fire for. Fate is a fickle bitch as I come face-to-face with a woman I thought I'd never see again.

Rose Marie Mariner, the sister of my ex-girlfriend. The ex who tore my heart to shreds, stomped on it, and left me, never to be seen again.

I'm not the only one in shock. Rose takes a step back when she sees me, her gaze flickering from me to Hammer, then back my way. Her gasp is audible as she covers her mouth with her hand.

"Didn't mean to scare you, beautiful. We're here to pick up the order for Priest. He ordered a bunch of flowers," Hammer says, breaking the silence and flashing his boy-next-door smile her way. Rose apparently realizes that Hammer has no idea we have history and takes a breath.

"Sorry, I'm not usually so jumpy," she murmurs.

"This is Thunder. He looks mean, but once you get to

know him, he's not all that bad." Hammer is flirting with Rose. This irks me. A lot!

Rose was the sweet sister. Clarissa was spicy. I fucking loved spicy over sweet. With Clarissa, everything was intense. She fucked hard, played hard, and lived life on the edge. She was passionate. Unfortunately, she was also cruel as fuck. You were only worth her time when it was convenient for her. When she needed money for clothes, or at least I thought it was for clothes, I gave it to her, only to find out she was buying cocaine and was an addict. I fell in love with her, or I thought I did. Maybe I just felt responsible that I was feeding her habit. By the time I figured it out, I felt used.

Still, I begged her to stop and offered to pay for rehab. Instead, she fucked me stupid, waited for me to fall asleep, took all the cash out of my wallet, and disappeared. Never saw Clarissa again. I went searching, partially because I was worried, but also because she fucked me over and I wasn't cool with that. When I said a lot of shit to her parents, Rose looked on from the other room, silently crying. I never saw any of them again.

That's when I decided that relationships don't work for me. I don't date. I fuck, and I fuck hard and fast. I make sure all the women know the score and that the time we spend together is enjoyable for both. I've never had any complaints. I love women and I like sex. I don't make excuses for who I am.

Rose grew up to be beautiful in every way, a dark beauty with eyes that shine brightly. Her lips are full and luscious, her cheekbones high, and her hair hangs down in one long braid. When I do a full-body scan, I can see that she has full breasts and hips. Her hourglass figure reminds me of an old-time Hollywood goddess. Clarissa was the exact opposite, blonde, with blue eyes and a feisty nature.

"If you'll give me a minute, I'll grab the boxes from the back," she says, quickly disappearing to the back room. Fuck me, even her voice is low and sultry.

"I'm happy to help you," Hammer says, but she's already gone.

I look Hammer right in the eyes and say, "She's off-limits." Hammer looks stunned. I'm not asking him to back off. I'm telling him.

We can hear her shuffling about, then she comes out a few minutes later with a box, leaves, and returns with another, then with a massive bouquet of long-stemmed pink roses in a crystal vase wrapped in cellophane. "They're already paid for. If you want to take these boxes out to your car, I'll put these roses"—she holds up the vase—"in a box to secure them better."

"That'll be good." I finally speak and motion for Hammer to make himself scarce. He picks up a box and takes it out to the truck. She hasn't given me a second glance, instead turning her attention to the flowers and making them perfect before she hands them over.

"Are you going to pretend you don't know me?" I ask, taking a step closer to her.

She lifts her head and eyes me cautiously. "It seemed to me that you didn't want your friend to know we had met," she replies, then goes back to what she was doing.

"How's Clarissa?" I ask snidely. I know I shouldn't be taking it out on her, but I can't seem to help myself.

"Clarissa passed away six months after I last saw you," she says dryly.

Now I feel like a shit! As much as I hated what Clarissa did, I wouldn't want that for her or her family. "I'm—"

"Don't say you're sorry. You shouldn't be sorry. She was terrible to you. She treated you badly and didn't warrant your pity. You should know that what she did to you, she did to all of us. My parents fought like hell to turn things around for her, but Clarissa never listened and wanted to live life on her terms. We weren't close, and I found out the hard way that she was only nice to me when she wanted something, but I wanted a sister so bad that I let her use me." She finally looks directly at me. "I just opened this shop a few months ago. People here are lovely. I'm hoping to be the florist of choice for the area. I don't want to have a problem with you, Michael." No one has called me by my name in years. Coming out of her mouth, it sounds nice.

She flits around, finding the perfect-size box and stuffing it with paper to keep the flowers secure.

"We won't have a problem, Rosie."

She stops what she's doing and flashes a shy smile at me. "Is Thunder your new name? Like Beyonce or Cher?" She's teasing me. I remember her doing that when I sat on the couch waiting for Clarissa to get ready for wherever the hell she decided we were going that night.

"Kind of."

She pushes the box toward me. "All ready. I hope she loves these."

"Quinn will love them."

"Lucky girl to have so many people to make her day special," she says. Maybe I'm imagining it, but her tone turns wistful, almost sad.

"How did Clarissa die?"

"Overdose," she says softly. "We were devastated. I'd like to say we were surprised, but we knew it would end that way if she didn't stop. She chose not to."

Hammer returns for the second box, and I grab the other. Hammer is about to leave when he turns and speaks to Rose. "I was thinking, maybe we can grab a coffee sometime."

I want to smash this vase right over his thick head. What did he not understand?

"Thank you, I'm flattered, but I don't date," Rose replies quietly. "Please give the happy couple my best."

What the hell does she mean she doesn't date?

As soon as we get out of the shop and into the truck, I turn to Hammer. "What the fuck was that? I told you she was off-limits," I growl.

Hammer grins. "I fucking knew it. You're into her."

I shake my head. "You're fucking crazy. I don't date girls. I fuck women."

"Yeah, she doesn't date either." Then the bastard laughs out loud.

I'm not ready to give an explanation to Hammer or anyone else. I feel like I need to protect Rose. The last thing Rose Marie Mariner needs is a man like me.

ONE

A Woman, Not a Child

ROSE

Never in my life did I expect to see Michael Donally again. He was so angry the last time he showed up at our house, I thought he was going to shake the door off the hinges with his violent knocking.

It was early morning when we heard the pounding. I jumped out of bed, hoping to get to the door before Dad, but he was already yanking the door open. We all expected to see a very high Clarissa standing there, and instead, it was Thunder, full of fury. Dad was stunned because Michael, or should I say Thunder, was always even-keeled. Any time he came over to the house with Clarissa, Thunder had been nothing less than respectful.

Even though I'm a wallflower, Thunder would find a way to include me in conversations or tell me jokes to make me laugh. I had a crush on him, hard. I knew he was with my older sister, but secretly, I wished it was me he wanted.

Everything about him was hot and still is. When I first knew him, his hair was black, with strands of red, which he wore up in a man bun. Today he wore it the same, but when he was dating my sister, sometimes he would keep it loose, and I would watch him ride off with his hair blowing in the wind. His eyes are so dark, in fact almost black, but they shine brightly when he laughs. Maybe it's because he's mature, carries himself with confidence, and knows what he wants that I find him so attractive. He was a no-nonsense kind of man. He said what he had to say and if he had nothing to say, then he wouldn't fake it.

What my sister did to him was horrible. I cringe at the thought of how it must have been to wake up and find your wallet empty and realize that the person you loved had abandoned you. Thunder was looking to build a life with Clarissa, and she threw that all away. And for what? Another hit!

What's worse is that she took Thunder away from all of us. My dad looked upon him as a son. My mother believed him to be everything a woman needed in a man: caring, attentive, and a great partner in life.

And me, well, I lost my best friend. He didn't know it, but he was. He was the person I felt free to be myself around. I told him stories about school and the dreams I had. He encouraged me, pushed me to keep dreaming, and taught me that I could do anything I wanted. My florist shop, Petals, exists because of him. This shop is what I've always wanted. When things got hard, I wanted to give up, but I kept hearing Thunder's voice in my head, telling me that I could do anything.

I both loved and hated my sister. I loved her because she was my older sister, and when she was younger, she was the coolest. Eventually, she turned into someone I didn't know. She was a user, and not just drugs. She used people, including Mom, Dad, her friends, and me. I could live with all that, but the way she lied and manipulated Thunder, that wasn't something I could forgive.

When Clarissa ran away, Mom and Dad were beside

themselves. I was relieved that she wasn't going to be able to hurt us anymore, and maybe Thunder would find peace.

It was four in the morning when a police officer came to the house to tell us they'd found a woman matching Clarissa's description in an alley. She had overdosed and was gone. We cried, we grieved. Although, I think each of us cried for different reasons. Mom because she lost a child and her thoughts went back to the sweet little girl Clarissa had once been. Dad felt like he'd let Clarissa down and that he should have been able to fix her. I cried because I was angrier than hell that she could do this to the people I love.

Mom and Dad are back in Nebraska now, where they chose to retire, surrounded by good friends and relatives. I go back as often as I can, but with the new shop, I'm here until I can hire staff to cover for me. My parents understand and support me.

I don't know how Thunder and I ended up in the same place, but I intend to stay out of his way. The last thing he needs is a reminder of the past. For my own sanity, I need to keep my distance. Thunder is far too hot to ignore, and I spent years when he was with Clarissa, watching him be the perfect boyfriend, knowing he'd never be mine. I don't think I could take seeing him with yet another woman on his arm.

Thunder

As I look around the room, all I see are Rosie's flower arrangements. They're unique, and all the women have commented on them, Ava especially, and she's already talking about visiting the shop in person. This doesn't bode well for me, because the minute they meet Rosie, they'll fall in love with her and want to make her one of the Lady Pride.

Quinn was surprised by the party and even more excited to see her family here to celebrate with all of us. Priest did good for himself. He and his sister, Camille, have come a long way in the last few years. Camille nearly worked herself to death and was being terrorized by her own family before Steady came into her life. Steady fell in love with Camille, and he didn't put up with her family tearing her apart and using her as a cash cow. She was going hungry to give them money.

Priest didn't realize to what extent he played into his mother's plan. When he found out how badly Camille was being abused, he walked away from his mother and everything she stood for. Guard, our president and sage, took him in. That was the best thing that ever happened to Priest. Shit! Finding the Pride has been the best thing that ever happened to any of the brothers.

Together, we're stronger. Each brother brings something to the table, and we would die to protect one another. That's just the way it is. It's a simple concept: respect, honor, and protect.

I came to the Pride from another chapter of the brothers. Guard was once part of their club before they asked him to branch out on his own. We knew each other back then, and I could see he was meant to lead. Guard wanted me to come with him, but I needed to roam the country first. I was restless, a nomad. I got bored too quickly and was looking for adventure. Guard told me to come find him when I was done. He said I'd always have a home with his club.

That was when I met Clarissa and settled down in a town that I thought was going to be my forever home.

Clarissa matched my zest for life. She lived free and hard. Then I found out that being free and hard to her meant getting high and doing stupid shit. I took her to rehab many times, yet it never stuck. I didn't understand it. Her parents fucking rocked. They were good people doing all they could to show their love for her. The more I tried to give Clarissa stability, the wilder she became, like a bucking bronco in a rodeo, not wanting to be tamed. In the end, she took off in the middle of the night. It wasn't the money she stole that pissed me off, it was that she couldn't be straight and tell me it was over. She played me.

Unfortunately, I took it out on the wrong people. I went straight to her parents and laid all my shit on them. They should have thrown me out or called the cops, but they didn't. They listened to me rant and swear and blame them for being crappy parents. It wasn't until Rosie stepped up to the door and poked me in the chest with her finger, telling me to shut my mouth, that I saw what I was doing to them.

"You're hurting, and I get that," Rosie said, "but so are we. You just told us that Clarissa disappeared. Do you have any idea what that does to my parents? Stop being so selfish and look around. As much as Clarissa doesn't deserve our love, she has it, and she knows it. You get to walk away and move on, but we can't because she's ours." Rosie was hurt, and I mean really hurt, and I just made it worse. She was right. I was only thinking of how I was feeling.

I did the only thing I knew how to do. I left. Years later, it isn't Clarissa who's haunted my dreams, it's Rosie. When I left, she was a kid. A sweet, soft, warmhearted girl. Now she's a beautiful woman who I can't get out of my head.

TWO

Not a Coincidence

THUNDER

It's been two weeks since I found myself face-to-face with Rosie, and since then, I haven't been able to get her out of my mind. I shouldn't care, but I want to know about her life. How are her parents? Where are they? They're good people. They opened their minds and hearts when they saw a rough biker at their door and didn't judge me.

Losing a child, no matter how much trouble she caused, must have devastated them. Erik tried time and time again to get Clarissa help. She had us all fooled. Made us believe that she was off drugs and wanted to live a clean life. Penny was so happy. She really believed that last time, it would stick and Clarissa would beat the addiction. She insisted on a special dinner with the family. I think we all bought into her act, except for Rosie.

I remember seeing Rosie that night, and though she's normally quiet, she was even more so that evening. I never gave it another thought, but her side glances at her sister weren't warm or accepting. They were fearful. I believe Rosie always suspected her sister was playing us.

This is the fourth time this week that I find myself at Hanna's Bakery and as good as her food is, my eyes are fixed on the flower shop across the road. The sign for Petals, in royal purple, with the P made to look like rose petals bordered in gold, represents what Rosie is all about. Rosie is delicate like the petals of a flower, but encased in a strong outer edge to hold herself up when things get hard.

Rosie comes out of her shop carrying a vase of flowers and walks across the street, heading this way. The ding of the bell above the door alerts Hanna, who is wiping off a newly vacated table. She turns to see Rosie standing there.

"Hi. I'm your new neighbor across the way. I hope you like tulips," Rosie says, extending the vase to Hanna.

Hanna smiles and takes them from her. "These are gorgeous. I love tulips. I've been wanting to come over and say hello, but things have been busy. My son, Romeo, has been sick with a stomach bug, and this is his first day back at school. Thank you for these. Can you sit for a while?"

"I should get back to the shop. I'm still new and can't afford to hire help yet. Soon, I hope," Rosie replies, holding up her hands and crossing her fingers.

"Oh! I remember those days!" Hanna says. "At least let me give you my special for the day to see you through. It'll take two minutes."

"Oh no, that's not necessary—" Rosie starts, but Hanna jumps in quickly.

"We small businesses have to stick together. Two minutes. Please?" Hanna rushes behind the counter, and as Rosie looks around, she finally spots me in the far corner near the window. I see her sharp intake of breath. Her cheeks turn pink, and her chocolate-brown eyes go wide. Damn, but she's beautiful.

"Hey, Rosie." Her eyes go soft when I say her name. I've called her Rosie since the first time I met her. She was a teenager when I met Clarissa. The two sisters were almost eight years apart in age. Rosie was an oopsie, unexpected, but loved. Clarissa would tease her younger sibling about how she had to make an appearance in the world and steal Mommy and Daddy's attention. That was far from true. Rosie was the independent kid, where Clarissa clamored for attention. On more than one occasion, I wondered if Clarissa did drugs to keep the attention on herself.

"Hi, Thunder," she replies. "Are—are you having a good day?"

A grin comes to my lips. She's always polite. "Yeah. I'd say so. How about you?"

"Really great. Since your friend ordered the flowers for his party, the shop has gotten a lot busier. One day, a group of women came in and almost bought out my entire stock for the day." Rosie laughs with her husky voice, and I swear it makes me hard. Fuck me! She's my ex's baby sister.

"I see the Lady Pride is on the move."

"Lady Pride?" she asks, tilting her head to one side.

"That what they call themselves. They're the wives and girlfriends of the Satan's Pride members. I'm a Pride." I point to my vest and the insignia etched into it.

"Are you happy?" They're not just words. I can see that she really wants to know.

"As happy as I can be. There are great brothers in the club. They're real family to me."

Rosie bites her lower lip. She undoubtedly remembers that I never had a family. My parents dropped me off at my grandmother's house and disappeared for days and weeks on end. They were more interested in their careers and traveling the world than looking after a kid. She died when I was fourteen, but instead of going to foster care, I took off. I was a clever kid and knew how to survive. The president of an MC took me under his wing. He was an older man, but he knew I needed guidance. He got me back in school and practically raised me. That's where I met Guard.

"I'm glad," she says quietly. Just then, Hanna comes back with a to-go box.

"Ham and Swiss with my secret spread. I hope you like tomatoes. And I added a little treat, a double chocolate brownie with caramel and pecan drizzle," Hanna announces as she hands her the box.

"Wow. This is too much," Rosie says.

"Please, I love my tulips. The girls come by for coffee around three o'clock tomorrow if you want to drop by and join us," Hanna offers.

"I'll try, but I'm on my own. Which reminds me, I have to get back. Thanks for this," Rosie says, lifting the box, then turns to me. "Nice seeing you again."

"Later, Rosie."

A couple of hours later, I found myself volunteering for a parts run. I hate deliveries, but this one means that I'll be driving by the flower shop around closing time. I sit in the truck as Rosie locks up and walks up the block.

I don't know what possesses me, but I follow her. I hop out of the truck, keeping my distance, watching as she moves up the steps of a cute cottage-like home and lets herself in. It's a small house, but it suits her personality, warm and adorable. The home is painted pale yellow, with a white picket fence and, of course, a garden full of sunflowers. They were always her favorite.

I stare for a little longer, but manage to tear myself

away. As I'm walking back to the truck, my cell phone dings.

A text comes in from Hammer. *Where are you?*

Be back in 5, I reply.

Seen Rose lately? he types back.

What the fuck! I look around as the truck comes into view. Hammer is leaning against the hood, along with Roscoe and Wildcard.

"Not a word," I warn.

Roscoe shrugs. "Don't know what you're talking about."

"Too bad the flower shop is closed for the night. I was thinking of picking up some flowers for Charli," Wildcard says with a smirk.

I glower at Hammer, who I presume is the one who mentioned Rosie in the first place. "I didn't say a thing. You can thank Hanna for that. She said there was enough electricity between you two, it could light up the whole town." I want to wipe his smug grin off his face, but instead, I pull open the driver's door, get in, and take off.

It can be hard at times when you're alone at the compound. Yes, we have our own rooms, but sometimes it's good to be able to roam. Unfortunately, the club is busy tonight. I decide to take a walk outside to clear my head.

When I see Rosie drive by and pull into a spot at Millie's Diner, I beeline for the diner as well. She's like a magnet, drawing me to her. The pull is so strong that I have to see this through. I'm not sure if it's because I was a complete dick to her and her family that last time I saw them, or maybe it's closure. I've mulled this over a lot since that day.

But as I see her sitting near the window, chatting with Millie like she was her new best friend, I'm thinking this isn't about closure, but the beginning of something. I must be losing my mind. This is Rosie. Sweet, innocent Rosie. Still, it's as if my body has a mind of its own, and I find myself walking into the diner and sitting down across from her.

"Wow. Twice in one day," Rosie says. Millie looks from Rosie to me, then back at Rosie and rolls her eyes. She's seen the mighty fall before. Guard, Orion, War, and the list goes on. Right here in this diner is where Orion and Vi fell in love. "From the first cup of coffee I served," is exactly how Vi puts it.

"Burger, fries, with extra pickles and a mega cup of java." Millie dictates my order. She knows me too well.

I glance up at her smiling face and show her my pearly whites. "Ah, Millie, you're the best."

"No need to butter me up. I already like you," she teases, then walks back behind the counter and into the kitchen.

"She's a hoot," Rosie says, still looking toward the closed doors.

"Millie's a good woman with a big heart. She's good people."

"This is a coincidence. Or maybe not. This is a small town."

"It's not a coincidence. I saw you coming this way and wanted to spend time with you." There, I said it out loud.

She shakes her head. "Is this about Clarissa? Because there really isn't much more to say."

"Clarissa isn't in this. She's gone. She's been gone for

years. You laid her to rest. I think it's good we let her rest in peace."

"I agree." She nods. "I don't want to bring up the past. My parents have been through enough. For months, people tried to get them to pay Clarissa's debts. Not collection agencies, but bad people. That was part of the reason they decided to move back to Nebraska to be with family. Dad's brother was the sheriff in town, and his son, my cousin, Andrew, followed in his footsteps. It makes me feel better knowing they have family around them."

"People threatened your parents?" I repeat incredulously. Fuck, I was so pissed at Clarissa and how she hurt me, I didn't think of anyone else. I got on my motorcycle and rode out right after my tirade at Erik and Penny. Fucking selfish! I was so busy licking my wounds that I never gave it another thought. I sure as hell would never have left if I believed they were in any kind of danger. God only knows the mess Clarissa got herself into. A junkie will beg, borrow, and steal to get their next hit, and sharks will go to any lengths to get their money back.

"Yeah, it got ugly for a while. Dad paid them, but they kept coming back. That's when he decided we weren't safe, because they would never stop." She sees I'm seething and rests her hand over mine. "It's fine now. Honest. Mom and Dad are with family. Dad and Uncle Will go golfing. Mom and Aunt Susan are taking a ceramics class together. They're enjoying their retirement."

"What about you? Those guys ever bother you?" I ask. I see by how she averts her eyes and pulls her hand away that whoever these assholes are, they did something. "Babe," I say, getting her attention, her gaze rising to meet mine. "What'd they do?"

"It was a long time ago. It's over," she says, trying to brush it off, but her expression shows that it scared her.

"Tell me," I say. She hesitates, sucking in air. "Rosie, either you tell me, or I'll go hunting for answers."

"Why? Why would you do that? We've all moved on."

"I've gotta know." I point to my gut. "In here. I feel it."

She folds her hands in her lap. "Fine." She closes her eyes for a second, and when she opens them, she blurts out, "They wanted me to pay back the money. They knew I didn't have the kind of cash they were asking for and told me that one sister was as good as another."

The burning in my chest just became a raging inferno. She was a kid, and those punks were going to make her into a prostitute. My expression must be murderous, because Rose leans in and takes my hand.

"It's the past. I ran home and told Dad. He got us out of there before anything could happen. We never looked back. Dad made me promise never to go back, not even to visit Clarissa's grave. I wanted to once, but Mom said that we could mourn her from anywhere. It didn't need to be by a grave site. I agreed, and that was the end," she tells me, even managing a small grin.

"I should have been there to protect you," I grit out through clenched teeth.

"Don't do that to yourself. It was a terrible situation that snowballed into an even worse one. You had every right to cut ties and move on. It's hurtful to find out someone you love isn't who they pretend to be. I'd had years of Clarissa's lying and manipulating. You didn't have a clue and trusted the woman you cared about. I knew she was going to disappoint you, but what could I do? I couldn't tell you. You'd think I was some bratty younger sister who was just jealous."

"I never loved her," I say.

Rose stares for a second, looking confused. "But—"

"I admired her fire. She was filled with dreams of

adventure, and I was entranced by her free spirit. I liked her. She was a lot of fun. She knew how to party, and you're right, she had a way of making people do what she wanted. When I finally saw her for what she was, I wanted to help her get better. I tried and tried. She shot me down or out-and-out lied to me. What we had was over long before it actually ended." I bare my soul to Rose, telling her what I've been holding in all this time. The guilt of staying when I was already mentally out of the relationship, and the guilt of not being able to see Clarissa's own worth.

"Whatever you had with Clarissa, even for a short time, it made her a better person. She was sick. Substance abuse is an illness. It was her decision to continue, despite the fact we all tried to help her. My father beat himself up for years over this. It ate away at him until he let it go." She squeezes my hand. "Please, let it go too."

I gave her the hard truth, and still, my Rosie is gentle with me.

Millie arrives at the table, clearing her throat to get our attention, holding two plates. We break apart as she sets them down in front of us. "You can reattach now," she jokes.

"Nah, I need two hands to grab my burger," I reply.

Rosie starts to laugh, bringing a smile to my face. "I'm glad this wasn't a coincidence. It's good to be around you again," she says quietly.

We eat and talk about where our lives have taken us since we last saw one another. Rose tells me about college. She talks about her dream to start her shop. Her parents aren't thrilled with having her so far away, but she was determined to spread her wings.

"Calls happen every Monday, Wednesday, and Saturday, with the occasional option of Sunday if they all get together and FaceTime to chat," she says. She talks about Ava and Vi coming in for a visit and how great they seem. It seems the Lady Pride have made multiple visits. Willow, Abby, and Izzy stopped by the other day as well.

"They're great. Ava is the leader in a sense. She's married to our prez, Guard. And don't let Vi fool you. She can be bossy, but she has a heart of gold."

"I sensed that. I love her style. They've all been super sweet. They want me to do lunch or coffee, but the weekdays are too hard. I'm barely breaking even and won't be able to hire for a while, but it's worth it. I love my little shop." She grins before taking another bite of her burger.

"You did a good job, although I was expecting fairy dust to drop from the ceiling. With my luck, I would have been turned into a toad."

"No way, silly. You can't turn a handsome biker prince into a toad. That's just not right," she says with a giggle.

Shit! This could be the beginning, if we can get past the past.

THREE

Saturday Night

ROSE

Time with Thunder is both wonderful and painful. Seeing him again, even as a friend, was just like it used to be, fun and light. After our heart-to-heart, we moved on to his time on the road and the colorful characters he's met. Thunder's always been all about seeing the world and meeting people.

He tells me about the club and how when he was ready to come back into the fold, Guard welcomed him with open arms.

"No questions asked. I got 'Welcome home, brother,' and that was it," he said. He explained the commitment of the Pride and told me about his brothers. Each one is so unique, and I was captivated by their stories.

I felt like I should have been taking notes, or that someone should write a book about the club and the people in it. When Thunder told me War is married to Maddie of the Smoking Guns, I nearly fell out of my chair. Maddie is one of my favorite singers and I have all her CDs. Then there's Risk, who's an incredible contractor, and he's married to Hanna. I nearly cried when Thunder told me about Hanna's ex-husband beating her. I wanted to hunt him down myself to teach him a lesson.

Thunder explained why they call Ava the queen of the club and how she put herself in danger to save Guard and the Pride. Starting over in a new town after losing her husband was difficult for her, but it seems that Guard set his sights on Ava and was relentless.

I'm not sure which escapade was more dramatic, Vi almost being beaten to death and Orion losing his mind, or Steady's wife, Camille, being extorted by her own family. She was rationing food while her mother continued to persecute her.

Each love story is more powerful than the next. Then finding out that Demon is Lucien Bardon, *the* Lucien Bardon, the famous rocker, made my jaw drop. I had posters all over my room of him and his group when I was a teenager. I gasped, and Thunder had to put his hand under my chin to close my mouth. The minute he touched me, no one else existed, not even the talented and superhot Lucien. That's all it took for me, one gentle touch from Thunder, and I was right back to the feelings I've locked away for so long.

When he walked me to my car, I was nervous because I wanted him to see me for me. The woman I've become, not the ridiculously shy baby sister of his ex-girlfriend. I swore for a minute he was going to kiss me, really kiss me. He leaned in, and I held my breath, waiting, then his lips found my cheek. His breath was warm, and the brush of his lips made my heart beat so fast, I thought I was going to pass out. It was over in a second, but the feeling of gushiness stayed in my belly all night.

In the cold light of day, though, Thunder is a nice guy who is making me feel welcome in his town. I'd rather have him as a friend than nothing at all.

In the shop, I go through my normal routine, turning on lights, my computer, and coffeemaker. I look through all the emails and prioritize the orders first. I'm holding my own financially. They say that businesses can take up to two years to turn a profit. I consider myself lucky that I've been able to cover the costs so far. Steadily the orders are picking up and the walk-ins are increasing daily.

It's time to put all thoughts of Thunder aside and concentrate on work. Fresh deliveries of flowers are set to come in within the hour, which means I need to make room for the new and create some bouquets and centerpieces with my current stock. I hate the idea of tossing flowers and will sell them at a reduced rate, hopefully tempting passersby to take them home to put them on their dinner tables.

Later that afternoon, elbow-deep in peonies, dahlias, miniature pink roses, and greenery, I look up at the door when the bell dings. Willow and Abby come through with several other ladies carrying trays of coffee from Millie's Diner and the beautifully designed box from Hanna's Bakery.

"Hi, Rose. I hope you don't mind us dropping in," Willow says, filled with sunshine. "Abby and I have been telling everyone about your place, and Charli, Sofia, Maddie, and Quinn wanted to see how amazing this place is."

I watch them file in and put names to the faces of the women Thunder spoke about last night. These women are beautiful. Sofia has an elegance about her, very tailored and put together. Such a different look from her rocker husband, Demon. Charli is fresh-faced and just has a natural glow about her. I know that she and Wildcard are a couple, and I hear that she's a wonderful fashion designer. If I remember correctly, Charli's father was trying to sell her off to some nasty people to whom he owed money. Quinn is tall and svelte, just like a model. I hear that she was Priest's saving grace. Priest's mother blamed Quinn for alienating Priest. His mother shot Quinn in her moment of hysteria, looking for Priest. But when Maddie walks in with her glorious auburn hair and rocker chick look, I'm stunned into silence.

"I think she knows who you are," Sofia says, laughing.

Maddie does a little wave. "Hi, Rose. Nice to meet you." She looks around my cute shop. "I love this place." Her eyes go to the newly put-together bouquet with hydrangeas and pink and cream roses. Her fingers delicately touch the petals. "This is gorgeous. Can I buy this one?"

I nod, still struggling to find my voice, but immediately regret my nod because I know the flowers will only last a few more days. "They're on sale. They won't last too long. I have new flowers in the back and can make you a fresh bouquet."

"All flowers should be enjoyed, and these will look perfect in my studio," Maddie replies, lifting the vase and holding it to her chest to take in their scent.

"Then you're in luck because I'm having a sale on everything in that section. Whatever is left over, I'm going to deliver to the hospital and senior center." I wave my arms to encompass the table I set up near the window.

Quinn peruses the table and picks out a lavender and cream array of flowers. "I'll take these, and I'll take two more, but deliver those to the hospital for me, please. If it weren't for them, I wouldn't be here right now with my new friend."

"That's an amazing idea!" Willow says, clapping her hands. "I want in on that." The others jump in, wanting to participate.

"That's very generous," I reply, a lump in my throat. This is the kind of town I've always wanted to settle in. A community where people come first and we're all working together. Respect and caring are the core values I grew up with, and through the years, I've discovered that these values aren't as common as it should be.

"I have an even better idea," Abby says. "I need to make a call and let you know if it all works out." She takes out her phone. Whoever is on the other end picks up quicky. "Hi, honey." A pause. "No, no, everything is great. I'm calling to see if you have a prospect or someone available to run some deliveries tonight. Rose has these gorgeous flowers she's put together, and she's working all day and plans on delivering the rest to the hospital or senior place. She'll be at it all night and, well, I was wondering if you or Guard could spare some time for a few hours." There's another short pause, then she turns to me. "He's checking to see who's available."

Sofia smiles and says, "Ghost will find a guy or do it himself. He would slay a dragon for his girl."

"Thanks, honey." Abby looks at me. "Wildcard and Roscoe have volunteered. They could be here in an hour. Does that work?"

"Wow, that's amazing. I don't know how to thank you," I gush.

"Are you kidding? You're the one doing all the work and spreading sunshine. It'll make a big difference to those places," Sofia says.

"Let's celebrate tonight. I think we should have ladies' night, and you must come, Rose," Willow says.

I've always had friends. I wasn't popular, though I was liked well enough, but there was never a real connection. Maybe because I was so focused on school, then on finding my own purpose, I never made those long-lasting friendships others talk about. But this feels right.

"I'd love that," I reply.

For the next hour, we sip coffee and eat our treats while I work. They all help where they can, and when Wildcard and Roscoe turn up, we all work together to load the truck. Before they leave, they tell me we'll meet at the compound to enjoy the evening, and to dress casual.

Five minutes after they leave, Thunder calls. "Hey, babe, I hear you've had a busy day."

"It's been an awesome day!"

He chuckles, and I can imagine the laugh lines around his eyes and the way his lips curl into a smile. Even over the phone, he makes me feel too much. "That's good. I hear you're joining us for our Saturday night shindig. I'll pick you up around seven. That cool with you?"

"You're coming to get me?"

"Yeah, babe."

"Um, yeah. That's cool." Is it cool, though? The more I see Thunder, the harder it is for me to handle what I feel for him.

Thunder

Rosie fills out a pair of jeans perfectly. She's ready and waiting for me. She always looks great, but with her hair fluffier than normal and wearing more makeup than usual, she's a knockout. I want to reach out and pull her into my arms and kiss her rosy red lips.

"You look great, but you better grab a jacket," I say.

"It's warm out."

"Yeah, but I'm putting you on the back of my bike."

Her eyes light up. "I'm getting a ride on your motorcycle? You've never let me ride with you. You said it wasn't safe."

"Now it is. Go grab a jacket." I watch her disappear down the hall, my eyes glued to her ass. She used to beg me for a ride. I wanted to take her, but the first time she asked, Clarissa pulled a face, and that was the start of our first argument. It was stupid, and that should have been a clue as to how much Clarissa resented her younger sister. Each time Rosie asked, I'd make up a new excuse. Then one day, she stopped asking.

Rosie comes back with a dark brown leather jacket, her brown ankle boots clicking across the floor.

"Is this okay? I mean for the club." She waves her hand over her clothes.

"Rosie, stop fretting. These people already love you," I tell her. I take her by the hand and lead her out the door. I slip the keys from her hand and lock up before walking her to my bike. The extra helmet I brought fits her well. I get on and hold out my hand for her. "Get on, babe."

I guide her on and let her settle in behind me. She wraps her arms around my waist without asking. She's in tight with her front to my back. I can feel her thighs pressed against mine. I close my eyes, reveling in the moment.

"Ready?" I ask.

"Absolutely!" she cries with enthusiasm, bringing a grin to my face. I pull out of the small driveway and head onto the road. The compound is close, but I decide that for her first ride, we're going to detour and take the long way over.

We drive through the scenic part of town and wind around the local park, then a little farther to the road leading out of town, where the rows of red and white oak trees are in full bloom, then back down toward the club. The club lot is full tonight. I guess they all wanted to party.

When I was younger, there'd be parties every night. Booze and biker bunnies abounded. We still have that, but not as often. A lot of the guys have settled, and the new recruits get enough action that they don't complain. Guard makes it pretty clear that joining Satan's Pride isn't about the pussy. This is about brotherhood first and foremost. It's about living life large, but doing it in a way where we're making a decent living and taking care of our families.

MCs can have a bad reputation, and at one time, the drug runs were a consistent form of income for the club. Guard wanted something different for this club. His dream was to legitimize our businesses and build a club that thrived without putting our lives on the line. We did that.

We're contractors, mechanics, cybersecurity, and more. Each members' talents are utilized, and we pool them all into a pot and divvy it out. None of us goes hungry, none of us will have to worry about money. Hell, I could retire tomorrow! Other clubs saw what we were doing and followed suit. Some decided they wanted a piece of our action. Guard protects this club, and since the brothers were all on the same page, we fought back.

Those MCs that came to take what's ours had a rude awakening. Satan's Pride didn't go soft, we got smart. We won't start a war, but we'll sure as hell end it. Our rivals learned fast enough not to fuck with the Pride. We've had some bumps in the road, but through it all, we've stuck together.

It's still early in the evening, which means the place is still rated PG. The party will rev into high gear later, but for now, we walk around back to the patio where the noise seems to be the loudest. Guard's in a group of men from another district, but he sees me coming and lifts his beer in our direction. I give him a chin lift and leave him to it.

Ghost is the first to greet us.

"Rose, right?" he asks. I gotta tell you that Ghost is as intimidating as they come. He's freaking huge and is overwhelming when you first meet him. Rose has to tilt her head way back to meet his gaze. I feel her stiffening beside me.

"H-hi," she manages to get out.

"This is Ghost, Abby's man. He's not nearly as mean as he looks," I kid. I see an expression of surprise when I mention Abby. I get it, though. Abby is very quiet and tiny in comparison to the mammoth giant in front of her. Abby comes to Ghost's side, and immediately, he tucks her into himself.

"I see you've met Ghost. We're so happy that you're here. We've been waiting for you. Most of us girls are over there." She points to the far end, where a bunch of lawn chairs are set up and a very giddy group of Pride women are sitting.

"Are they smashed?" I ask Ghost.

"Not yet, but they will be. I have a feeling a bunch of us will be spending the night," the big man says with a chuckle. "It's Izzy and Saint's turn to watch the kids. And I think Camille and Steady are going to head over later to help out."

"The kids?" Rose asks.

"The little Pride, I call them." Abby giggles. "We have Gavin and Ryder, who belong to Ava and Guard. Vi and Orion are parents to Gabby and Alexander. Romeo belongs to Hanna and Risk. Camille and Steady have the cutest little guy named Kyrian. Who am I forgetting?" She taps a finger to her chin. "Oh, Maddie and War have sweet Amelia and baby Adam. They won't be staying either because she can't bear to be away from him overnight yet. Not that I blame her, he's so darn sweet." Her voice goes higher when she gets excited. "I'm stealing her for a while," Abby announces, practically dragging Rose over to the others.

"Don't fight it, man," Ghost says as Rosie looks back at me over her shoulder.

"Who knew Abby could get feisty?" I tease.

"That's what happens when she's had two appletinis, apparently. I can't wait for later when I can get the best use out of her feistiness."

I grab a beer and mingle, with one eye constantly looking over at Rosie. She seems to be having a good time. She has the same laugh as I remember. It comes straight from her belly. It's real, not forced. I'm glad that she likes this crew, because if I have my way, she's going to be here a lot.

A couple of times, I catch her watching me. She waves or lifts her martini glass my way, with a sexy smile on her face. I'm going to have to make my move soon. My dick is already straining against my jeans, and I've taken way too many cold showers in the last couple of days.

The music gets louder as the night wears on. The girls move to the makeshift dance floor on the grass. They're dancing and singing to Demon's new hit song. Demon is roped into the mix by his wife, her arms around his neck as she gazes up at him adoringly.

I'm not a dancer, never have been. It's not until I notice a guy from the visiting club making his way through the crowd and heading straight for Rose that I decide I need to stake my claim. I slide in behind Rose and wrap an arm around her middle. She lets out a startled squeak, turning her head to see it's me.

Rosie relaxes in my grip, but I'm still staring at the guy

who was coming to make his move. He gets the message, nodding his head and giving me a two-finger salute. My eyes move around the room until I find Hammer, who is outright laughing at me. I should go punch him in the mouth. He called it right from the start. Guard is next to him, looking pretty smug too.

"Aren't you going to dance with me?" Rosie says, turning in my arms. The music has changed to a slow song. Her hands slide up to my shoulders as she sways to the beat. I move with her, my hands at her waist, instinctively pulling her closer.

She gazes into my eyes like she's trying to figure me out.

"Do you know what's happening here?" I ask.

She releases a heavy sigh and murmurs, "I'm not sure."

I lower my head and brush my lips lightly over her soft, trembling ones. "What about now?"

"Thunder—" she says breathlessly.

"For you, I'm Michael," I whisper in her ear.

"Are you sure? I mean, there's so much history between us." Her voice is filled with concern, but I swear there's also a hint of hope, which gives me the boost I need to keep going.

"A lot of history was good, some not so great, but you've always been Rose and I've always been Michael. Two people searching for what makes us happy. Let's enjoy the night. I'll take you home and we can talk some more, or I'll leave you to think on your own. When you're ready, all you have to do is call."

She opens her mouth to speak, but the alarm on her watch starts flashing. She glances at it and shrieks, "My shop is being broken into!"

Her terrified expression says it all. I get it. She's invested everything into Petals.

“I’m on it,” I say. Taking her by the hand, I call out for Ghost and Guard. “Rose’s store alarm has gone off. I’m going to check it out and could use some backup.”

Ghost rounds up Hammer, Wildcard, and Roscoe. They race over to follow us out while Ghost explains the situation. Guard tosses me the keys to his SUV. “I’ll meet you there,” Ghost shouts as we take off.

FOUR

The Break-In

THUNDER

"Stay in the car," I command. "Lock yourself in." I wait for the locks to click before approaching the shop. Hammer and Roscoe are with me, while Wildcard has gone around the back. The front door is ajar, and the lights are all on. The place is in shambles. Potted plants lie on the floor, with dirt splattered all over the floor. The cooler glass has been smashed and broken flowers are strewn on the tiles. They've been trampled and aren't salvageable at all. Worst of all, there's a message spray-painted on the wall. *Found you. You owe us.*

Wildcard comes in through the back. "They were in and out fast," he says. "Got some tread marks. Risk and Saint are better at tracking. We should get them involved."

Roscoe's over by the cash register. "It's empty," he tells us.

"Shit! She's going to freak the fuck out," I grit out. I stomp out of the shop and see Rosie staring from the car. She unlocks the door and runs toward the shop. I stop her before she can get past me. "Slow down, baby."

She eyes me cautiously and does a deep swallow. "It's

bad," she whispers, looking past me and in through the window.

"Yeah, Rosie. It's bad. But you need to know I got you covered," I say. "How much did you have in the register?"

She shakes her head. "Not much. I keep a couple hundred for float. I use the nightly deposit slot at the bank."

"That's good. Really smart." I hug her closely. She's shaking in my arms.

"I need to see it," she murmurs.

I want to prepare her for what she'll see. "The place is a mess. This wasn't about the money."

"Vandalism? But why? I don't know anyone in this town besides you guys. I'm nice to all my customers, and they've been super great to me. Who would do this?"

I've got an idea, but I don't want to say it out loud. Her parents moved to get away from the scum Clarissa owed money to, and I have a feeling they found Rosie instead.

"I'm not sure yet, but Risk and Saint are great trackers. They'll get a lead from what we find. I don't want you to touch anything until we've done our thing. Okay?"

"I have to clean up. I need to make a living. I have loans to pay." Her voice grows louder, panic starting to set in. "Oh my God, I'm already running tight on cash. I can't put out any more money. I can't ask my parents for help. They're living off a retirement income." She's hyperventilating.

"Hey. Hey. Stop! We'll figure this out. We'll get this place fixed up tomorrow, and you'll be open in a few days. Do you trust me?" I ask, tucking my finger under her chin and lifting her gaze to mine.

"Yes."

"That's right. I've got your back. Take a deep breath, calm down. Then I'll take you in."

She inhales and exhales slowly, once, then again, closing her eyes. When she opens them, she sounds steady and calm. "All right. I'm ready." She holds my hand, squeezing it. "Lead the way, big man."

Rose

I try to hold myself together, but one look at how my cute, little shop was trashed and I fall apart. Thunder holds me in the back room as I let the tears flow.

"I worked s-so h-hard. It took me years t-to save up to start my shop," I sob into his shirt.

"You're killing me, babe," he murmurs in my ear. "I hate seeing you cry like this." He strokes my hair soothingly.

"Sorry to interrupt," a voice says. We both look up to see Risk at the door.

I gather myself together, grabbing a tissue and wiping my face. Thunder waves him in. "What's up, brother?"

"I know this is a lot, Rose, but I need to know if you have any other surveillance cameras besides the one aimed at the register."

"No. I didn't think I'd need another one. To tell you the truth, the only reason I got that one was because my insurance company said it would make my payments cheaper."

"Rosie, you have insurance," Thunder states with a grin. The lightbulb goes on, and it dawns on me, I have insurance. I'll be covered for a good portion of the damage.

"I have insurance!" I shout gleefully. Then I remember how long it takes for them to get this done and my smile disappears. "It takes them forever to get the paperwork started. I can't afford to wait that long."

Risk turns and calls out for Demon, who appears in the doorway.

"What's up?" Demon says. I still can't believe that Demon, the man covered in tattoos and piercings, is the same Lucien Bardon who was part of a rock group years ago.

"How's Sofia with moving along an insurance company to pay out?" Risk asks.

A devious smirk rises to his lips. "Have you met my pit bull? Get me the information and policy number, and she'll be on it."

Guard must have been listening in on the conversation at the door and pops his head in. "In the meantime, the Pride will float you the money to clean this up. Risk will do the repairs with his crew, and you can pay him when the insurance company cuts the check." Just like that, he disappears without waiting for a response.

I glance up at Thunder. "It's too much. I can't let you all do that."

"Babe, Guard's made up his mind. There's something you gotta know about the Pride: you don't fuck with our family, and you're family."

I want to tell Thunder that I love him. That I've loved him since I first saw him walk into our house. That for years and years, I tried to forget him, but he was always in my heart. I never expected to see him again, and now to have him and to feel the warmth of the people he calls family and to hear that they consider me one of their own is overwhelming and beautiful. I can't seem to get the words out.

Instead, I come up on my tiptoes and kiss him lightly on his full lips, his whiskers tickling my skin. "Thank you."

FIVE

Danger Lurks

THUNDER

You can hardly call her lips touching mine a real kiss, and yet it's making me feel more than I ever have for anyone. The need to protect her is fierce.

The note on the wall tells me this isn't a random act of vandalism. She's already told me how they tried to shake down her father for money and how they approached her at school. Clarissa's past was darker than I thought. I have no idea what kind of mess she got herself into, but now it's affecting Rose and her family.

I need a meeting with my brothers. They need to know what they're dealing with. Based on how they've reacted tonight, they'll do what they do best, take care of their own. No matter what, Rose won't be left to deal with this alone.

I'm not sure what the future holds for Rose and me, but I know I have to find out. There are good memories and bad ones, and I have no idea about what she thinks about Clarissa and me having been together. But the truth is, Clarissa is dead, and we were done even before she left. The feelings between us weren't there anymore.

I often think about why I stuck that relationship out so long. I convinced myself I had a responsibility to try to help Clarissa, but she didn't want the help. I knew it was a losing battle. Change only happens when you want it. In the end, I stayed because I loved her family. Penny and Erik treated me like a son. Erik and I would sit on a Saturday or Sunday afternoon and watch a game, while Penny would fuss and feed us.

While Clarissa would be sleeping off the effects of whatever the hell she was on, Rose would sit with Erik and me, cheering for her favorite team or yelling at the referee for a bad call. Rose was a completely different person when her sister wasn't around. She was vibrant and funny. As soon as her older sister walked in the room, it seemed like she disappeared, melding into the furniture.

For a time, I wondered if Rose was comparing herself to Clarissa and thought she would never measure up, but now that I think back, it was because she didn't like the drama. Clarissa would tease her sister over anything and everything. Rose distanced herself from her sister out of self-preservation. I read the situation wrong. Now I'm thinking there's a lot more to Rosie than I realized, and I want to know it all.

When I'm sure that my brothers have the shop sorted out, with Risk boarding it up until he can get to it in the morning and Demon and Saint gathering clues as to who did this, I suggest that I take Rosie home.

Rosie is reluctant, saying, "I should be helping."

"They're almost done for the night. Tomorrow we'll come back and help. You need to sleep and so do I." She nods, thanking all the guys for what they've done.

We drive the short, few blocks to her home in silence. Her eyes are drooping. She's wiped. Understandably so, with the chaotic day and even crazier night. I walk with her to the door, taking the key and letting us in.

"Stay here," I tell her as I go through each room of the tiny cottage. This place is as neat as a pin. It's filled with candles and warm, rich, inviting colors. The sofa is the kind you can sink into and let the day's stresses disappear. "It's all clear."

This is where I should say goodbye and let her go to bed, but I notice how she's tensed up. There's no way she's going to be able to relax.

"I'm pretty tired. Do you mind if I crash on your couch?" I ask.

She takes a step forward. "I know what you're doing," she says with a sad expression.

"Let me do it."

"You won't get any sleep on that tiny couch. Take the bed. I'll sleep on the couch."

"No fucking way that's gonna happen."

"What? Why?" she asks, lifting her shoulders to her ears.

"In the first place, this is your house, and in the second, a man doesn't take a woman's bed. That's just not right."

"We can share the bed," she says, then quickly adds, "It's a big bed. We can sleep, uh, you can sleep, um… we can—"

I could have let her go on because she's absolutely adorable when she's flustered, but I give her an out. "Sleep is good. We can both use the rest. Why don't you go first? Get changed and ready for bed. Holler when you're ready, and I'll come in."

Her cheeks turn a bright pink, and she bites her lower lip. "Okay." She brushes by me.

I stop her and hold her for a moment. "There's no pressure between us, Rosie. I want there to be an us, I make no pretense about it, but it'll happen when you're ready." I drop a chaste kiss on the top of her head. "You're safe with me."

"I've always felt safe with you. Always," she says, then heads to her bedroom.

I take my time locking up the house and looking around her place. The kitchen is a soft country blue and white, with a retro feel. It suits Rosie. I remember how much she loved working in a kitchen. She liked to cook alongside her mother.

There are pictures on the far wall, mainly of her parents, some of Rosie with her friends, and one of Rosie and Clarissa. They were much younger in this photo, both girls smiling as the camera snaps the photo, Rosie looking over at her big sister adoringly. There was a time when Rosie looked up to her sister. By the time I arrived on the scene, that was far from the case.

Hearing her call my name, I walk down the hall. I tap on the door to let her know I'm coming in. She's sitting up on one side of the bed with the covers tucked around her waist.

"I took out a spare toothbrush for you," she says, pointing to the small bathroom off to the left.

I make quick work of washing up and come back. When I take off my shirt, Rosie diverts her gaze. Then I take off my boots and jeans and slip in beside her. "Turn off the light, babe." She does as I ask, and I listen while she settles between the sheets. I lie on my back and sling an arm over my eyes to try to drown out the fact that the most exquisite creature is beside me and it's taking all the control I have to hold back what I really want to do.

Her breathing steadies. She's asleep. As I'm about to

doze, she turns in her sleep, and I find her tucked into my side with her arm around my waist as she buries her face in chest. Christ have mercy. It's bad enough to take in the scent of her perfume, but to have her body pressed up to mine is sheer torture.

I count backward from a thousand and finally fall asleep, while tightening my hold on Rosie to keep her close.

Rose

T*he next morning…*

Thunder is in my bed, pinning me down with his arm. If it weren't for nature calling, I'd stay in this position all day. I carefully lift his arm, slip from the bed, and go to the bathroom. Despite the terrible event of last night, I managed to sleep well.

I saw the message on the wall in the shop. I knew immediately that this wasn't a random act. I was targeted. All because my sister was a crackhead and who knows what mess she left behind. I have no idea how many thugs she owes money to or how much. In a country this big, I moved to a small town to live a quiet little life, only to get sucked into the vortex of Clarissa's disastrous trouble. Even from the grave, she's causing me grief. Thunder tried to downplay it. He said the culprits may have been trying to scare me. Unfortunately, I know better, and I'm convinced this could be the same bunch of hoods that came to visit after Clarissa died.

The thought of being alone in my house was scaring the heck out of me, so when Thunder offered to stay, I was relieved. I shouldn't be a coward, but I'm happy he stayed and not only because of the break-in, but also because I like him in my house.

A pang of guilt hit me at the thought of Thunder trying to sleep on a tiny couch, and when I offered to share my bed, I stuttered like a foolish schoolgirl. I dreamed so often of having him in my bed. Thunder is handsome even asleep. His face is serene, but his chiseled features are prominent. He's got a strong chin and high cheekbones, and his beard only makes him look more badass.

When I come back to the bedroom, Thunder is sitting up in bed, shirtless. His yummy abs are on display and I'm gawking, yet I can't help myself.

"Rosie, you keep looking at me like that and I'm not going to wait for you to say you're ready for me," he teases, the sexy grin on his luscious lips only making me want to jump him.

"You're hot," I state. Maybe it's stupid to lay it all out, but I've never played games before, and I don't want to start with Thunder.

He raises his brows. "Glad you think so, babe. So why are you standing all the way over there?" He jerks his head my way.

"I know stuff about you."

"What stuff?"

"S-sex stuff?"

He furrows his brow, tilting his head to one side. "Sex stuff?" he repeats. "What kind of sex stuff?"

"Clarissa talked about you. And…she said things about…you." I finally get out the words, looking down at my bare feet, unable to meet his gaze.

"What did she say?" When I don't speak, he holds out his hand. "Baby, come here." I go to him, and he tugs me down to sit on the edge of the bed by his hip. "I have no idea what Clarissa told you, and it pisses me off that she would say anything at all. I know that girls talk and shit, but you were a kid compared to her. So, yeah, I want to know because I can see this is worrying you."

I'm so embarrassed. I can feel the heat rising to my face. But Thunder's right. If there is to be an us, I have to be me and say what I feel. "She said you liked to be rough." I peer up at him through my lashes. "Really rough. Like choking and stuff…" My voice trails off.

He sighs heavily and looks to the ceiling, then back at me. "First, I don't get off on hurting women. What your sister and I had was about what worked for us. She wanted it and I gave it like she asked. No two relationships work the same. Didn't enjoy it then, and never, fucking ever, did I hurt her. Do you believe me?"

Without hesitation, I say, "I believe you. I've only had one boyfriend, and I could never compare what I felt for him to what I feel for you."

His face relaxes, although I can see he's still pissed about it. "I want to kiss you, but I won't, because our first real kiss isn't going to be tainted by the past. So instead, you're going to give me a minute to get over the overwhelming urge to throw the lamp across the room and get dressed, and I'll meet you in the living room."

I giggle because I know he wouldn't throw a lamp and he's trying to lighten the mood. "I'll make coffee."

"Don't bother. I'm taking you to Millie's for breakfast. We'll make plans for the day from there."

Not fifteen minutes later, a young man called Noah drops by with a change of clothes for Thunder. We talk for a bit, and I find out that he's Charli's younger brother and a prospect with the club. He's a great kid, and the way he talks about his sister, you can tell there's real love there. Noah's helping out at the mechanic shop as well as going to school.

You can see how he looks up to Thunder by the way they interact. Thunder has that way about him, where people can just be themselves. While the two have a chat, I run in and take a quick shower and get dressed for the day. I still have to tackle the cleanup at the shop.

Thunder

I don't like it, not one little bit. From the time Rose and I left her place and got in the car, I've had an uneasy feeling, like needles prickling down my spine. A red Corvette was idling four houses down from the house. First off, red Corvettes in this town are as rare as they come, and when I drove by, I made a point to stare the driver down. What I saw in the eyes of the dark-haired punk, I didn't like.

He knew I was on to him and disappeared down the other side of the street. I've already made a call to Guard about meeting this afternoon at the club with the brothers, but now there's more to tell. As Millie serves our meal, I notice another vehicle that doesn't belong. It sits by the curb, but the driver keeps looking into the diner.

There are too many coincidences, and all of them tell me that danger lurks nearby. It's broad daylight, and in this town, you'd have to be an idiot to try something, because it's a fact that the people here care about each other. But I know better than to go against my gut.

"Don't move from this spot, babe," I tell her.

"Pardon?" She blinks at the harshness of my tone.

I reach over and touch her hand. "Promise me to stay put. I've gotta make a call."

"Okay," she whispers.

I notice her concerned expression. "You're safe with me." I wait for her to nod, then pull out my phone and walk to the door.

The phone rings once, and Guard picks up. "I feel it, brother." I don't know how he fucking does it, but he can sense trouble and is on it faster than lightning. "Where are you?"

"Millie's."

"I'm sending War over. Come back to the compound, make sure Rose is with you. Charli and Willow are around and will keep her busy while we meet."

"They want Rose."

"They want a war, we'll give it to them," Guard responds.

SIX

Yours and Ours

THUNDER

Rosie isn't happy knowing that we're heading to the club instead of the shop. She wants to get Petals up and running again as quickly as possible.

Risk overhears her and calms her fears. "My crew is already on the job. The place will be cleaned up by end of day, and I'm going over later on to make a list of what we need to get it back to its former state, sparkling lights and all."

"I should be helping," Rosie counters. "You're all working, and I'm doing nothing."

"It's easier if the place is empty for us to work," Risk says with complete honesty.

Charli offers a way to keep her busy. "Let's make a list of the stock you need to replace. We can get that on order today and be ready to go when Risk and his team is done."

Rosie seems satisfied with that plan. "That's true. I'm going to be spending long nights getting floral arrangements together. I just hope I haven't lost the interest of my regulars." She sighs. I leave her in good hands with Willow and Charli. Both women have been instructed that Rose isn't allowed to leave without me.

What most MCs call "church," which is an official meeting of the members, we call the "round table," like in the knights' tales. It started off as a joke, but it makes sense for our club. We ride free and live free, but we're not out to hurt others. We're actually well-liked by the people in this town. The town of Bournham was dying. All the viable businesses were shutting down and the young people were leaving for greener pastures. Guard started off with a parts store, and we've expanded to include a ton more resources, which meant jobs for the town.

The club is growing too, and we're going to need to expand this room if we keep adding new members. It's standing room only, with the original members sitting at the table. War, Orion, and Demon are among them, and of course, Guard, who stands, waving me forward.

"Floor belongs to Thunder. Go ahead, brother," he says.

I look around the room, but before I can speak, Demon says, "Whatever you need, I'm in." I smile at the depth of his loyalty, and the room erupts with the same message. I wait for the clamor to subside before I say my piece.

"I appreciate it. But I think you need to have all the information first. Then if you still want to help—"

"We're in, man," War says. I look at the mighty warrior. There's no other way to describe him. He's big and he's a mean motherfucker if you cross him.

"All right. Rosie is the sister of a woman I dated way back. Clarissa was a lot older than Rose, and when I met her, she was full of life and a lot of fun. She was also a great liar, and she knew how to hide her shit. I found out she was a junkie. Her parents were out of their minds with worry. Together, we put her into rehab over and over again. One night, she fucked me over, stole from me, and took off. I lost my shit on Rose and her family before leaving town. I thought that was it."

"What about Rose?" Risk asks.

"She was too young back then. Did I feel something for her? Yeah, but it felt wrong. Especially having been with Clarissa."

"What the fuck is happening now?" Saint asks.

"They're together," Hammer says.

"The night I saw Rose again, I knew I was fighting a losing battle. It seems that she's thought about me the same way I did her. We're still figuring it out, but I want to make her my old lady," I say.

"And the shop?" Risk asks.

"That's where this gets messy. Clarissa died of a drug overdose six months after I left. Then, Rose and her family were shaken down for money that Clarissa owed. It got to the point that Erik, Rose's father, had to move the family back to Nebraska. I think what happened last night involves the same group of men that Clarissa was involved in. The message on the wall indicates that's the case. And this morning, there was a red Corvette waiting for us, and then at the diner, another car had eyes on us. None of this feels right."

"Does Rose know who they are?" Steady asks.

"Nah, the last time they came to her, she was in college and her father got her the hell out of there. I'm going to call Erik myself and see if he has anything else for me."

"So, these guys are shaking down a woman who had nothing to do with her sister's crap? That's cold," Wildcard says. This hits too close to home for him. Charli was basically thrown into a similar situation.

"What's the plan?" Saint asks.

"Orion's doing a search on the license plate Thunder

picked up today. Risk is working at getting the shop back in order. Demon, I need you to work the streets for information. War, Steady, and Roscoe, I need you on security duty. The rest of us will all have to pitch in as well. The work needs to continue. Come see me after to get your assignments," Guard announces. He pauses for a moment, then adds, "These aren't just thugs. It's bigger and uglier. I've already spoken with Risk. He's going to help us get in touch with the Viale brothers. Ghost and I are going to see if we can get a little help from them. I got a feeling this is more than a drug deal gone wrong."

I'm stunned by Guard's words. I know what's happening isn't good, but for Guard to ask for assistance from the Viales heightens my angst. It's a blow to my gut, and all I can think of is keeping Rose safe.

"I'm not leaving her alone until this is over," I state firmly. Guard nods.

Ghost adds, "Didn't think you would. Although, she might start wondering just how bad this is."

"Rose is aware these guys are nasty. She was around when they threatened her parents. Which means they could be in danger too," I surmise.

"He's right," Orion says. "Do we have anyone out that way who can keep an eye out?"

Saint steps forward. "I know a guy. Name's Hawk. He's solid, smart, and his club works like ours. A brother from the special ops."

"You're sure he'll do it?" I ask.

"Calling him now. If I know Hawk, he'll have men on their way before I get off the phone," Saint says with a chuckle.

"I'll owe him," I say.

"We'll owe him," Ghost replies. "Rose is yours, so she's ours."

SEVEN

I'm Not Scared

ROSE

The afternoon went by so quickly that I didn't even get a chance to go to the shop to see what was salvageable. I wanted to push for Thunder to take me, or even drop me off and I'd find my own way back, but the minute he came out of the room with the rest of the club, I knew better than to ask.

When we're alone in Thunder's car, I finally have the courage to ask.

"Can you drop me at the grocery store? I had shopping on my list of things to do, or the only dinner we're going to have is peanut butter and jelly sandwiches, and even that's a stretch. It might be on crackers," I say, hoping to elicit a hint of a smile. That failed miserably.

"We'll make a list, and one of the guys will drop it by," he replies, never taking his eyes off the road.

"It's a lot of stuff."

"Won't be a problem."

"Thunder, pull over." I've had enough of the short answers that are hardly answers at all.

He glances over at me. "What?"

"Pull. Over," I state more sternly and clearly. He veers off to the shoulder of the road and turns to me. "What's going on? And don't say nothing. I know it's not nothing, and once more, this is happening to me, so I ought to be involved."

"The people who did that to your shop aren't punks on a spree just out to create havoc. I don't want you to assume the worst, but we're playing it cautiously. That means random trips to the store are something we can do without. The Pride is on it. We've got men looking into Clarissa's past acquaintances, and Orion's doing an internet dive. But you mean something to me. It took us years to get to where we are, and that means I'm not going to lose you now. I'm sorry if I'm freaking you out, but I'm not leaving your side until we've got this wrapped up."

I'm both happy he's being honest with me and scared out of my mind that these are the same guys. All of a sudden, my parents come to mind. If they found me, they'll find… "Mom and Dad?"

"Already taken care of. We have a sister club out that way. They're jumping in to help. Their president, Hawk, has already got your parents on watch."

"He does?"

Thunder reaches out to cup my cheek. "I get that this is a lot to take in. And I promise you, when this is all over, it'll be nothing but a story to tell our kids, but for now, I need you to stick with me and our plan. Can you do that?"

The warmth of his hand on my cold cheek is comforting, as I lean into it. "I can do that." Our kids! Did he just talk about telling our kids stories? My heart melts and I can imagine a little boy with a wild sense of adventure, a carbon copy of Thunder, running around and getting into mischief.

"Let's get home. Make a list, and we'll get what we

need. Tomorrow, I'll take you to the shop so you can see that it'll be up and running in a couple of days. Sofia and Demon are coming over later to catch you up on the insurance stuff."

"Already?"

"Babe, Sofia is a badass bitch lawyer when she needs to be. She doesn't waste time," he says. I blink. I can't imagine Sofia being anything other than sweet and gentle. "The club has her on retainer for a reason, even before she got together with Demon."

He restarts the car and takes us home. Just as he said, Roscoe picked up the list and was back within the hour with everything that I wanted. I thought Roscoe was leaving for the night, but then I saw him sitting outside in his car.

"Why is Roscoe still outside?"

"Protection, Rosie."

"Is he going to be there all night?"

"Nope, Hammer will be taking over later," he says without batting an eye.

"Should we invite him in for dinner?" I ask, not knowing the biker protocol for protection duty.

Thunder laughs. "Yeah, sure. If you want. I've never known Roscoe to refuse a meal."

"Don't laugh at me. I've never needed guarding before. I don't know how this works," I say, exasperated.

He comes farther into the kitchen and braces his hands on other side of me, against the counter, closing me in.

"You're cute," he says. "And sweet. And funny. Everything about you makes me want to kiss you senseless. I haven't laughed as much in years as I have with you in the last two days. I would kiss you, but that means that dinner is going to go to shit. This is the plan: I'll get Roscoe, and we'll eat. When Sofia and Demon are gone, I'm going to finally get the taste of Rosie that I've been dreaming of for years."

I swear my panties are wet. I want to toss the spaghetti and meatballs out the window, then call Sofia and tell her to come tomorrow because I want his kiss so badly. He touches his lips to the hinge of my jaw, then leaves to call his brother for dinner.

All through dinner, I think about his promise in the kitchen. It's a good thing the guys were involved in their own conversation and my sparkling wit wasn't necessary. I could barely touch my food, but the way Roscoe and Thunder inhaled it, I assume it must have been good. I like to cook. It's something I find soothing. I'm not nearly as good as my mother, but I try very hard.

"A good sauce is what makes the meal," she used to say when it comes to pasta, and she's right. Pasta is pretty plain until you dress it with the right combination of herbs and tomatoes, then the simplest of meals turns into an explosion of flavor for you to enjoy.

Roscoe is an easygoing guy with a big heart. Willow told me about how he worked hard to put his sister through school on his own. I ask Roscoe how he and Willow met, and he replies, "I was forced off the road, and these men who were pissed that I took their friend back to jail were coming back to finish the job, when a golden-haired angel came to my rescue." The story gives me goose bumps. Roscoe is as protective of his girl as Thunder is of me. And when it comes to Willow's safety, Roscoe doesn't take any chances. I can see why she is head over heels in love with him.

I'm serving dessert when the doorbell rings. Sofia and Demon have arrived.

"Tell me there's more of that," Sofia says, her gaze fixed on the bowl in front of Roscoe. He moves it closer to himself, digs his spoon in, and takes a bite.

"I made a mixed berry crumble. There's plenty for everyone," I tell her with a grin. I get two more bowls and fill them.

"Let's sit on the couch," Sofia says, leaving the guys at the table. Once we take a seat, Sofia takes a bite. "Mmm, this is heavenly. This is as good as Hanna's."

"That's high praise. Hanna's desserts are the best I've ever tasted."

Sofia pats my knee, a soft, reassuring touch. "How are you doing?"

"Truthfully, this has me a little rattled," I admit. "I poured my savings into Petals. My life was finally where I wanted it to be."

"You'll get that back," she says, sounding very sure of herself. "I've had a chat with the insurance company, and they're cutting a check in a couple of days. I sent them Risk's estimate. They balked a little, and then I sent them two other estimates that were significantly higher, and suddenly, they agreed to pay out. I'm having a courier pick up the check to make sure they don't delay the process. That much is taken care of."

"They never work that fast. I've heard stories of people waiting months before they get a payout," I say in astonishment. "You're a miracle worker."

She laughs. Sofia is beautiful, but she's more than that. She's kind and generous. I've heard Demon talk about all the pro bono cases she's taken on for those who can't afford legal counsel. I also know that she volunteers at the youth shelter once a month.

"No miracle, just common sense," she says.

Feeling close to Sophia in that moment, I tell her something I haven't told anyone else. "I loved my sister, but I hated what she did to our family," I whisper. "She didn't only destroy her life, she was slowly killing my parents. Mom cried every night she didn't come home. Dad waited up in a chair until all hours of the night, only after cruising the streets looking for her. I saw what it did to them. It was awful." I pause, my lower lip trembling. "Do you know what it's like to be woken up by a police officer at the door telling you that they found your sister dead in an alley? I should have felt something other than anger. I was so mad at her. I'm still angry for what she did to our family. Then to have men show up at the house and harass Mom and Dad for money… A lot of money, I might add. That was the last straw. I just stopped feeling for her."

"She was sick. Addiction is an illness. It's hard to find your way out," Sofia says, taking my hand.

"You have to want to find the way out. She didn't. Clarissa wanted instant gratification. It was all about her. She was the golden girl. She was beautiful and smart. Then slowly, she become a person no one recognized. It was so ugly near the end, before she left, that I couldn't even stand to be in the same room as her. What does that say about me?" I sniffle.

"It says that you loved her a great deal. No one has those kinds of deep emotions unless they love the person. You couldn't watch her continue to hurt herself, and you did the best you could in a very difficult situation. Self-preservation is what you needed to do to keep yourself sane." Sofia squeezes my hand. "You did the right thing for you. No guilt. No shame."

"She died alone. Like trash in an alley," I whimper, the memory causing an ache in my belly. I wipe away tears.

"Perhaps. But her life had meaning," she says. I raise my eyes, furrowing my brow, urging her to continue. "She brought Thunder into your lives. Maybe that was her purpose. When Demon came into my life, we played it off like it was a fling. It wasn't until some nasty people put me in the hospital that he realized we'd almost lost each other. I'd take that beating all over again, as long as we ended up together."

"Don't fucking say that again, Fi. I never want to see you hooked up to tubes again," Demon grumbles. The men make their way over to join us. Demon takes a seat next to his wife, wrapping an arm around her shoulders. Automatically, Sofia leans into him. They're perfect together.

Thunder sits in the armchair next to me, his gaze fixed on me. He heard me talking about Clarissa. I'm pretty sure Demon noticed how quiet Thunder has become as well, because he stands to excuse Sofia and himself and says goodbye to us all. Thunder and I walk them to the door. I give Demon and Sofia both one last hug as they leave. Roscoe files out after them, reminding us he's on duty until Hammer comes in for his shift.

This leaves Thunder and me alone, with the promise of a kiss, but he doesn't make a move. I busy myself bringing the dirty dishes into the kitchen and loading the dishwasher. I can sense that he's watching me. The silence is so thick that it unnerves me. I whip around and ask, "What's wrong?" I clutch the dishcloth in my hand, wringing it tightly.

He looks worried. He opens his mouth, but nothing comes out. Then he finally says, "I don't want to frighten you off. I've wanted this for so long. You've wanted this for so long. It should be perfect, and all this outside crap is feeding into what should be the perfect moment."

Oh God! He hasn't changed his mind! I drop the cloth on the counter and race toward him. He's caught by surprise as I leap into his arms, wrapping my legs around his waist. He quickly grasps me as I lower my forehead to his. "I'm not scared. I'm grateful you feel the same. Please kiss me." I barely get the words out before his mouth is on mine. This isn't just a kiss. It's a dedication to what we mean to each other. His mouth is needy and demanding. I want to give him everything, anything. His firm lips mold to mine, licking, teasing, nipping. A surge of electricity pulses between us, and soon, a kiss isn't enough. We both want more.

"I need you, Michael. Please," I beg breathlessly. He pulls my head back down to his lips and carries me off to my bedroom.

EIGHT

All My Nights

THUNDER

There's a sizzle when our lips meet. Her arms lock around my neck like a vise, her legs around my waist, and her heels dig into my back. A kiss isn't enough. We're both greedy for more. When Rosie runs her fingers through my hair, tugging at my scalp, my desire ratchets up until I can't deny my need to be inside her.

"I need you," she murmurs, her husky tone only makes me harder, and my cock is already straining against the zipper of my jeans. I carry her through to the bedroom, where I drop her onto the bed, then climb in, my knees on the mattress. I reach out for her and tear at her clothes, just as she does with mine as our mouths connect.

Before we know it, we're naked and breathing hard. I need to slow this down, or it'll be over far too fast.

"We've got all night, Rosie," I whisper into the crook of her neck. "I want to take my time."

She stares at me wordlessly with those chocolate-brown eyes. I lay her down on the soft mattress, allowing myself to enjoy the view of her long dark hair splayed over the white sheets. Her creamy white breasts are heaving. I run my hands over her flushed skin, over the pebbles of her nipples, which tighten under my touch. I follow the curve of her waist and hips and down her outer thighs, watching her shiver with excitement.

I take a nipple into my mouth, then suckle lightly while I play with its twin. She holds my head to her chest, arching her back. I move her hands from my hair, placing them on either side of her head, and lift my head.

"Keep your hands right here." I watch as she grips the sheets, licking her lips. My mouth traces a path around her nipples, then lower over her belly to the top of her mons. "Ready for more?" I ask, our eyes locking.

She nods, and moans, "Yes."

I nudge her legs apart, then wider still. Her pussy glistens with moisture. All I can think of is wanting to taste her. I kiss the inside of one knee, then the other, and make my way upward toward her core.

"Michael, you don't have to," she murmurs.

"Oh, I have to," I tell her, then slip my tongue over her clit, eliciting a primal groan, her lower half jerking up. I place my hand on her belly to hold her still, my shoulders keeping her legs open as I indulge in the delicious taste of her wetness. I let my tongue slide over her pussy, my fingers spreading her lips open, and I eat like a man who's ready to devour his favorite meal. I circle her clit with my tongue and insert two fingers inside her. With every lick and push of my fingers, her moans grow louder and more labored. I keep pumping my fingers inside her. She arcs and moans, her breasts jutting out. Her legs tense as she comes for me. Her eyes are hazy and her voice is raw as she cries out my name over and over.

I come up on my haunches, grabbing for my wallet and pulling out a condom, thankful that I remember when all I want to do is get inside my woman. I align my cock at her entrance, taking a deep breath to force myself to go slow. I'm a big man, and as much as I want to thrust inside to assuage the ache between my legs, I go nice and slow. I swear, the look on her face as she takes my cock is an aphrodisiac like no other. The way her breath hitches with every inch I slide into her brings me closer to my own end.

"Oh God, yes," she says, lifting her hips for me. Watching my cock disappear in her pretty pussy makes me want to pound my chest like a caveman. When I'm fully in her, I wait patiently for her to catch her breath. It's not until she wriggles beneath me that I know Rosie's ready for more. I edge out halfway and thrust hard and fast.

She meets me thrust for thrust, her hips gyrating, her hands clutching my shoulders, begging so sweetly for me to let her come again. I give her what she needs, what we both need. Within seconds, she comes apart in my arms as another orgasm rocks through her core, and I roar my own release.

Rosie murmurs something incoherent as I gently move out of her and lie down beside her, gathering her in my arms. I pull the covers up over us, cocooning her in next to me. With her head on my chest, she looks up.

Her lips are swollen from our passionate lovemaking, her eyes look at me adoringly, and her warm pliant body is molded to mine. A woman content and satisfied. Christ! I've never seen anything so beautiful. I've dreamed of Rosie just like this. Convinced myself it would never happen because the past was too ugly. Yet, here she is, sleepily closing her eyes, with an arm slung around my middle as she burrows closer.

"Rosie, are you awake?"

"Mmhmm?" she murmurs.

"This is important, baby. Are you listening?" I murmur

into her hair. She stirs and forces her eyes open. "I want all your nights. They're all mine, do you hear?"

She nods, a crooked smile on her face. "You have my nights and days, for as long as you want them."

"That's right. You're mine."

With that, her eyes close, as do my own. I listen as she sleeps. The situation has changed. I would have fought with my last breath to protect Rose, but now failure isn't an option. If anyone touches her, I'll kill them.

NINE

Pimps and Mafia Links

ROSE

The next morning, I wake to find Hammer in the kitchen with Thunder, sipping coffee. There's an overnight bag by the front door, and as I walk into the room, Thunder looks my way. Hammer follows his gaze, a smug grin on his face as he elbows Thunder in the ribs.

"Come here, babe," Thunder commands. I go straight to him, and he greets me with a hard swift kiss, then he whispers in my ear, "You look good. Too good. I'm not going to be able to let you out of my sight."

I lean into him, but say to Hammer, "Hi, Hammer. How's it going?"

"Fine as can be," he says, taking another sip from his cup. He looks so much like a poster child for the army, with short, well-kept, dark brown hair, deep brown eyes, and a lean, muscular body that I'm sure could crush any opponent. He's a boy next door with an edge. His clean-shaven face shows off his dimples. I'm sure he doesn't want for female companionship.

"Want me to get you a cup?" Thunder asks, lifting his

own mug. I steal it from his hand and take a sip of his coffee.

"Nope. I'll just share yours." Thunder chuckles, and it's one of the most glorious sounds I've ever heard, almost as sexy as when he groans my name during his orgasm. I can't make a spectacle of myself with Hammer in the room, so instead I ask, "Are you staying awhile?" I jerk my head toward the bag.

"That's the plan," Thunder says. "There are two options, babe. Either you move to the compound, or I stay here. Either way, you're not alone until this is done." His fingers run up and down my arm.

Some women would find his no-nonsense behavior aggressive or controlling, but I know Thunder. He's an alpha male, absolutely. Controlling, never. I find I like that he's protective. The fact that he has great friends who he considers brothers and who are ready and willing to jump into the fire with him says a lot about him.

"I like my cottage," I reply.

"Then we're here," Thunder confirms. "We can have breakfast and then head over to the shop."

"Are you in the mood for pancakes?" I ask.

"I'm cooking."

"You're making me pancakes?" I tease.

"Omelets," he says, turning his back and rummaging through the cabinets. He takes out a frying pan, then moves to the fridge to get the ingredients he needs.

"Damn! He likes you a lot," Hammer says. "He doesn't make omelets for just anyone, you know."

"If you shut up, smartass, you can stay, and I'll make you one too." Thunder laughs at his friend.

"Hell, yeah." Hammer sits his ass down across from me at the kitchen nook. Hammer is very open about himself. He tells me about his time in the army and how he came to become one of the Pride members. He talks about his sister, Izzy, who is married to Saint. Saint is a doctor and runs the clinic in town, and Izzy is a teacher at the local school. There's no doubt that he loves his sister, his parents, and his Pride family.

It feels good to laugh. Hammer and Thunder are easy-going and banter back and forth. When we're done with breakfast, Thunder drives me to my shop. Risk's done an amazing job so far. The mess is gone. The holes in the walls have been repaired, and it's nearly restored to its previous state, only better.

"The new cooler arrives today. I've got an electrician coming in this afternoon to install it. Two more days and we'll be done," Risk tells us.

"This is incredible." I scan the shop, and I daresay it looks cleaner and more modernized. Much better than before they trashed it. "I have a new shipment of flowers coming in very soon. I can't believe you did all this." I reach up and drop a chaste kiss on Risk's cheek. "Thank you."

"That's the only one he gets," Thunder rumbles, hooking an arm around my waist and pressing his lips to my temple. I can see that he's kidding by the glint of mischief in his eye.

"The insurance will cover most of it. Can I work out an installment plan for the rest?" I ask Risk.

Risk looks stunned. All right, an installment plan won't work. I'll have to dip into the last of my savings. "Is she kidding?" Risk says, directing his question to Thunder.

"Nope." He sighs.

Risk turns his attention back to me. "We worked with what we had. The biggest part was removing the mess. The rest is really optics. The Pride is taking care of that.

Your only real cost is the plumbing and electricity to bring the place up to code and put in the new cooler."

"That's too much," I protest. "You've been here nonstop and putting in way more hours than normal. Your men need to be paid. You shouldn't be out of pocket for that."

"You don't have to worry about that. I always take care of my crew." He glances back to Thunder. "She's cute." He chuckles, walking away and shaking his head, but still smiling.

"What's cute about wanting to pay someone for the work they've done?" I ask.

"You're mine."

That's his answer, and I have no idea what that has to do with anything. "How is that an answer?"

"That means you belong to the Pride. All these guys did was help family. Family doesn't pay one another. One day, Risk will need a hand, and I'll be there. Or Hanna might need you, and I know you'll be there for her too. Simple as that." He shrugs like this isn't a big deal.

"I wasn't yours when this happened," I remind him.

"You've been mine since the day I walked into the shop with Hammer. No doubt about it, baby. I fought the pull of you for two and a half seconds, then went all in."

I flatten my hand on his chest. He covers it with his own. I've spent years dreaming of a moment just like this, and there's so much I want to say, but saying anything at all seems unnecessary when I feel his heart beating in unison with mine.

Thunder

I leave Rosie with Risk when Guard calls and asks me to meet him and Orion at the club. I know she's in good hands, yet I'm still reluctant to leave her. Rosie is busy decorating her new shelves and seems to be focused on her task.

Before leaving, I kiss the shell of her ear and murmur, "Take it inside. Risk is keeping watch and I'll be back soon."

"You got it, Captain," she says with a sly grin, giving me a salute.

It's a short drive to the club, where I find Orion and Guard waiting for me in Guard's office. From the stack of paper spread out on the desk, I can see that Orion's been busy.

"How's Rose doing?" Orion asks.

"Better than I thought. I think seeing her shop ready to reopen soon is distracting her from the other shit."

"About that other shit, Orion's dug deep. Maybe you can help make sense of this," Guard says.

I nod and take a seat next to Orion. He picks up some papers from one of the piles, rummaging through to find a photo. "Does this guy look familiar?" Orion asks. I look at a mug shot of a man who resembles a street hood. He wears his oily slicked-back hair in a ponytail, has close-set eyes and a crooked nose. He looks like he's been in too many street fights. Yet, I don't recognize him.

"No. Should I?" I shake my head.

"Think back, man. Maybe hanging around Clarissa?" Orion says. I study the photo again, but I get nothing.

"Sorry, no. Who is he?"

"He was a local pimp from the same city Rose and her family lived in when you were dating Clarissa," Orion says.

"He's now deceased," Guard adds.

"Murdered," Orion continues. "They never found the killer, although I don't think the police looked too hard. John Harvey pissed someone off pretty good. He was shot execution style, telling me this was a mob hit."

"What's this got to do with Rosie?"

"Clarissa was working for John Harvey. She was his prize prostitute. After she left town, she hooked up with this guy and turned tricks. Clarissa was arrested several times in the time she worked for Harvey, and each time, he's the one who bailed her out," Orion tells us.

"I had Demon get confirmation from his people," Guard says. "It's all true. Harvey kept her in one of his apartments with an ongoing supply of drugs. Demon also found out that Harvey's girls were taken over by the same mob family that killed Harvey. It seems that when Clarissa found out that Harvey was dead, she stole money from his safe. Money that belonged to the mob."

"You're thinking these men tracked Rose down and want her to repay what Clarissa took," I finish for them.

"So far, that's what it seems," Orion says.

"Who are they?" I ask.

"We're not sure yet. I've got Reno checking it out. He promised to get back to us as soon as he knows anything," Guard says.

"Can't we put word out there that Rose is under Satan's Pride protection?" I ask.

"Already done. But that doesn't guarantee these guys will back off. Until we know who they are, we need to stay vigilant," Guard insists.

"How the fuck did Clarissa get herself caught up with a guy like that?" I rant. "She had everything. Her parents were there for her. They were present for everything. Erik nearly lost his mind when he found out Clarissa was using. They took her to rehab repeatedly and stood by her side every step of the way. They weren't rich, not by a long shot, but Erik made sure his family had all they needed. How could you throw all that away?"

"It's not about her parents or Rose." I hear Demon's voice. He's standing by the door. "My parents loved me. The world loved me. But I didn't love myself. The problem began with me and ended with me. It starts off with just wanting to feel good. Then it turns into wanting to forget the bad days. Before you know it, it's always a bad day and you can't get through any other way."

"You got clean. You fought," I remind him.

"Deep inside, I didn't want to die. I wanted the noise in my head to stop and for the world that I was part of to disappear, and I didn't know how to make that happen without cocaine. Guard was at the right place at the right time and gave me a place to call home. There was solace, peace, and you all gave me purpose. But the decision not to die that night was mine. I don't know what Clarissa's demons were. You don't either. And we can discuss what a waste it was to lose her, but that's not going to change the fact that she's gone or how she left this world. And I would concentrate on Rose. She's still angry with her sister. That's not healthy for her or for you. It's not your job to fix her, but you and I both know how unhealthy anger can be."

Demon's recovery from his drug addiction is nothing short of a miracle. A rich rock star loses his best friend and bandmate and he spirals out of control. He went from legend to loser in one fell swoop. His courage and tenacity to claw his way to where he is today is impressive, to say the least. I take his advice seriously.

Demon is right. Rose is my priority. I can't let my own past cloud my judgment on Clarissa's choices. My parents didn't even want a kid and made sure I knew it every fucking day of my life. I left home as soon as I turned eighteen and never looked back. I wasn't physically abused. There was food on the table or in the cupboard. I had my own room, but that was where it ended. I was a stranger living in a house with two adults and I was cramping their style.

I call my parents on all the designated holidays. Mother's Day, Father's Day, and Christmas. I don't know why, but I do. The conversation is always brief, and when it's over, I'm more pissed off than ever. Not once in all these years have they asked me to come home for a visit. I keep telling myself that I'm not going to place another call, but I do it anyway.

Demon's words are ringing true. Perspective is key, and I'm grateful he's taken the time to enlighten me.

"Thanks, brother." I pat Demon on the back. "I appreciate it. I'll keep an eye on Rose and find the right opportunity to see if she's ready to talk about it." He nods and gives me a brotherly slap on my back.

"I actually came here to let you in on another piece of information." Orion's and Guard's ears perk up.

"Whatcha got?" Orion asks.

"Harvey wasn't just a pimp and a drug dealer, he was linked to the mob," Demon says. "He was transporting drugs across state lines for them. It's what got him killed. That night, three guys were found murdered in a warehouse. One was Harvey, and the other two were part of Harvey's crew. Everyone thought it was a turf war, when it was about Harvey's pissing off a local mob boss. Along with getting rid of some of the drug competition, the new Mafia clan took over their business enterprises—and they're collecting on all the debts."

"We're on the right track. For now, we're in a 'wait and see' position until Reno gets back to us," Guard says. "We hold steady."

"Any word from Hawk? Has anyone been out to see Erik or Penny?" I ask.

"All clear, but Hawk's got them on his radar and eyes are on them twenty-four seven until we work this out," Guard confirms.

Hawk's a good man. He and Guard are cut from the same cloth. At one time, it was a toss-up which club I was going to call home. It's becoming clear why I'm meant to be with the Pride and the brothers, since this is where Rose settled.

"I can't believe the circumstances have gone from pimps to Mafia links," Orion mumbles. "Is life supposed to get any easier at some point?"

Our club has been through our fair share of turbulent storms in the past, between rival gangs, insane gun-wielding family member, and crazy exes, and this isn't the first run-in with a Mafia family either.

"We can handle it," Guard states with steely determination, resting a hand on Orion's shoulder. "If you can handle that fiery wife of yours, this should be a piece of cake," he jokes, lightening the mood. We have a good laugh, mainly because Guard's assessment of Vi, Orion's wife, is dead-on. Sweet as sugar on the inside, she's all fire and attitude on the outside.

TEN

Stick with Me

THUNDER

Rosie is wiping down shelves and placing new vases and trinkets on them, creating a romantic display. When she hears the chime over the door, she looks over her shoulder.

"How does it look?" she asks.

"Looks good, babe."

"I'm going to make this a wedding nook. A place where a couple can come in and look at flowers for their wedding day. I'm going to add a small white table and a couple of chairs. I've done a few weddings. I'm going to add the photos to a photo album. That way, the couple can get some ideas." She steps off to the side where a wall unit stands. "And here, I want to display specialty items that can be added to flower arrangements for special occasions."

"You've been busy," I comment with a smile. I glance around. "Where's Risk?"

Risk's voice booms from the back. "Right here. I got eyes on her. We're installing the cooler." He sounds strained. I walk back to find him hefting one side of the large unit, while a guy who I assume is the electrician navigates his way behind it.

I rush to Risk's aid, calling out, "Over here, Rosie."

She comes immediately. "What can I do?" she asks, hand outstretched to help.

"Nothing, but I want you where I am." Am I being paranoid? Maybe, but my gut says to keep her close.

"Lady, can you pass me that wrench by your foot?" the man says, pointing to her feet. She picks up the wrench and hands it to him. "Two more minutes and this is done. Then I can work alone."

When we're finally done, we leave the guys to finish the job. Rosie goes back to fussing with the limited stock we were able to salvage, while I pull Risk to the side to fill him in on my discussion with Orion, Demon, and Guard.

"Reno will come through," Risk says. "Sebastian and Dante will be on it, especially Dante. You know these guys won't let us down."

"Yeah, but how long will it take before Rose breathes free?" I say. Risk glances at Rose, who is humming and completely oblivious to our discussion.

"She good, man. She's not feeling it. She may have been in shock when it first happened, but she's dealing with it. Rose is stronger than you give her credit for." He sighs. "I know what you're feeling."

I raise my brows in silent question.

"My wife was being robbed blind by her ex-father-in-law. And that was after she endured years of abuse from her ex-husband. Hanna suffered for years. When I found out, all I wanted to do was wrap her up in cotton and keep her away from the ugliness of the world," he says. "Hanna refused to cave. I still don't know how she found the courage, but she's still standing. Rose has fight in her too, and with you by her side and the Pride behind her, she's gonna be fine."

I point to my temple. "Here, it makes sense." Then I put my hand to my gut. "Here, something's not right."

"Proceed with caution, pay attention, and remember you're not in this alone. Either of you," Risk says, then goes to check on the cooler, coming back a few minutes later. "It's done. It'll need the night to get to the right temperature. Final touches will be finished in the morning, and we're done. Hanna would like you to come over tonight for dinner," he says to Rosie and me, adding, "Romeo hasn't seen his Uncle Thunder in a while," as incentive.

"You good with that?" I ask Rosie.

She nods. "I can't bring flowers. I don't have any yet." She surveys the room, frowning.

I bend my head to her ear. "She likes red wine."

Rosie perks up and smiles.

Rose

There's not much more I can do at Petals until the shipment comes in tomorrow. Then I'll be up to my eyeballs in work. It'll be good to get back into my shop. Before we left the shop, I grabbed a wine holder made to look like a birdcage.

While Thunder was getting showered and changed, I placed the bottle of red wine we picked up, along with a box of Baci chocolate on the table, tying a blue-and-gold ribbon around the neck of the bottle. I'm putting the final touches on the bow when my cell phone rings.

It says unknown number, but I pick it up anyway.

"Hello?" I say tentatively.

"You owe me," a low, scary voice says.

"Who is this?" My hands are shaking, and I'm frozen in place. I grip the phone harder to steady my trembling hands.

"Your new owner," the heinous voice replies, riddled with scorn and ugliness.

"What?" I cry, trying to understand what he's talking about. Then the phone is removed from my hand, and Thunder has it at his ear, listening to the caller.

"Listen, asshole. Rose is a Satan's Pride, and you are in for a world of hurt." That's all he gets out before the click on the other end tells him the caller hung up. Thunder holds me to him. He must feel the shivers running through my body. He soothes me with his loving words. "You're safe, Rosie. No one is gonna get anywhere near you. I've got you, baby."

"He said he owns me. He actually said he's my new owner." I look up at him pleadingly. "What does that mean?" My hands fist into his T-shirt. He doesn't respond, but holds me tighter. "He's not going to stop, and I don't even know why."

"He won't have a choice. I'll find him, and when I do, I'll tear him limb from limb," Thunder growls.

"Why are they doing this?" I whimper. "These are the people Clarissa got involved with, aren't they? I didn't want to believe it. I hoped it wasn't, but it's them."

Thunder doesn't bother lying. "Yeah, baby. It's them." He drops his chin on top of my head. I'm holding on to him as tightly as he's holding me.

Eventually, he guides us to sit on the sofa, nestling me into his side, and pulls out his own phone.

"Shit just got worse," he says into the phone, after which he follows with a couple of grunts of "Yeah" or "No problem," before hanging up and calling Risk to let him know we aren't coming and quickly explains why.

An hour later, Hanna and Risk show up at our door with Romeo and enough food to feed twenty people. At first, I'm not sure that I'm up for company, but Hanna has a way of calming the ripples of the emotional tidal wave I'm experiencing. Soon, we're sitting around the living room with plates on our laps, watching Romeo have a deep and meaningful conversation with Thunder about the new truck he got from his parents.

Romeo is a serious boy, as are his thoughts. You can see that he thinks about what he wants to say before speaking. He's a smart little thing. I love that he's inquisitive and asks a lot of questions, although I can tell his parents have their work cut out for them. A simple answer isn't enough. Romeo wants to understand the "why" in the answers.

Thunder already explained to me that Romeo was adopted, but I swear he looks like Risk and has some of Hanna's mannerisms. I believe that being a parent isn't just about genetics, it's about love. Romeo is a happy, loving boy who has adapted to the love and respect that Hanna and Risk show him, and Romeo gives it right back.

"Are we having a sleepover?" Romeo asks.

"Not tonight, buddy. One day soon, Rosie and I will have you come and stay overnight," Thunder tells him.

"And Gavin?" he asks. Romeo talks about Gavin a lot. It's clear these two are besties.

"We'll have to ask Uncle Guard and Aunt Ava," Thunder says.

"Ryder will want to come." Romeo pouts.

"Don't you like Ryder?" I ask.

"Sure, but he likes to play fight, and I don't like it so much."

"We'll just have to tell Ryder that there's no fighting at my house. I don't like tussling either."

The little guy gives me a giggle. "Tussle," he repeats.

Darn, he's so cute that I want to snuggle him hard. It's as if he knows what I'm thinking, because he walks right into my embrace, wrapping his arms around my neck and hugging me close.

All a sudden, all the bad stuff from the day is wiped away with the warmth of his snuggle.

Thunder

Even with my Pride brothers having Rosie's house on watch, I had a difficult night sleeping. I only got the tail end of the call. The douchebag's intimidation tactic shook Rose up pretty good. I know I'm going to have to tell Rosie everything we've found out, about her sister and the depths of her involvement with John Harvey and his gaggle of whores.

It's not something I want to do, yet Rosie needs to understand the dangers involved. I can't delay it any longer.

"Babe, come sit for a minute," I call to her as she finishes loading the dishwasher.

She glances over her shoulder. "We need to get to the shop."

"The shop can wait a little longer. Your delivery isn't due for another couple of hours."

She studies my face, then slowly comes over to sit

across from me. I reach out to take her hand. "What is it?" She sighs, preparing herself for more bad news.

"Clarissa was into pretty bad shit."

"I know."

"Really bad, babe."

She squeezes my hand and says again, only louder, "I know."

"You may think you know, but it's more."

"More?" Her brows rise, and her tone sounds more dejected. "How much more can there be?"

I tell her all about John Harvey and his association with the Mafia. Then I explain her sister's role in Harvey's life. I can see that some of what I'm saying, she's already surmised, but the part about the mob boss and the extent it played into the death of Harvey and maybe her sister is news to her.

"The mob is after me?" Her voice is a high-pitched shrill.

"The mob is after money owed to them," I correct.

"I don't have any money. Clarissa never came home after she left, never gave me or Mom and Dad anything. She was an addict. If she ever had money, it would have been pissed away on heroin." Her face turns red with fury. "Even in death, she comes back to make my life a living hell. Most sisters play Barbies together or have secret midnight gab sessions about boyfriends. But not my sister! No, she had to snort, shoot, and drink herself to death, then suck everyone else into the vortex of the insane underworld."

Rose stands and begins pacing the room like a caged tigress, continuing to rant, throwing her hands up and looking to the heavens for enlightenment. She drops her hands on her hips, leaning forward. "What am I supposed to do? Oh! I know," she says sarcastically, "I'll wait for the next phone call and calmly tell the man, who wants to kill me, or worse, make me into a prostitute, that I'm not interested." Her chest heaves with anger, desperation, and fear.

"Rosie. Calm down, baby." I grab her hand and pull her between my legs. "None of that is happening. Risk knows some people who are working on getting a name. Once we know who we're dealing with, the rest will work itself out."

"He says he owns me. I didn't understand what he was talking about until this moment. He wants me to—"

"It ain't happenin', babe."

"I don't want you or the guys to get hurt. Maybe, I should run—"

"Don't fucking finish that sentence. You run, I'll follow."

"But—"

"No buts. Together, with my brothers, we're stronger. You run, and we're out there alone. And before you start freaking out about your parents, we've got an ally club on it. They're being watched, and so far, no one's showed." I give her a gentle shake. "Stick with me, Rosie."

"Okay."

I give her some time to let all I've told her sink in. This is a lot to take. Even as a teenager, Rosie was a sensible, level-headed person, but throw this kind of disaster in her path and she has every right to be rattled. The mere mention of the Mafia would have any normal person shaking in their boots.

A while later, as we drive to the shop, Rosie puts her hand on my knee to get my attention. I glance over, and in a quiet voice she says, "I trust you." I lift her fingers to my lips and kiss the back of her hand, putting it back on my knee and covering it with my own hand.

ELEVEN

The Bloody Message

ROSE

Once we get to the shop, we see the workmen packing up the last of their stuff. Risk is inside checking it all out one more time. He's thorough and takes pride in what he does. Thunder explained that Risk wanted this business, and the club backed his idea, knowing he was going to make it a success. Satan's Pride is part owner, and this construction business has made them all very comfortable.

"All done. I hope you're happy, Rose," Risk says, coming out of the back room.

"Happy? I'm ecstatic! I can't thank you enough for everything you've done. As soon as the insurance money—"

"Yeah, yeah. Don't worry about it," Risk says, cutting me off. "I know where to find you." He winks. "I'll just look for Thunder," he teases. Risk looks to Thunder. "Noah needs some extra cash for school. I thought I'd send him over. You down with that?"

"Sure. We could use a hand to get the shipment off the

truck and into the shop. That way, Rose can concentrate on what she does best," he replies.

Risk departs, leaving Thunder and me to wipe down counters and shelves to make room for the delivery. Noah arrives not long after we start, just in time for a large truck to pull up.

Roses, dahlias, peonies, luscious greens, and much more begin to fill the empty spaces. Petals is alive with color again. The only time we take a break is for lunch, when Thunder sends Noah over to Hanna's to pick up some sandwiches.

Some of the Lady Pride drop by to help out. Camille and Abby come by to help me put together a few bouquets, but before I can even put them in the window to sell, they buy them themselves.

"This store is dangerous," Camille says. "I can't seem to walk away without picking up some fresh flowers." She giggles, and Abby joins in.

"I know what you mean," Abby says. "I love this vase." She picks up an ice-blue vase with a gold leaf design in the center.

"That would look wonderful on the fireplace ledge," Camille urges. "With pink roses."

I can't help myself; I take three large peonies and mix them with purple lilacs and arrange them in the vase, adjusting them just so. I add a little boxwood greenery, and by the time I'm done, I'm loving it and decide to make several others similar to the one I completed. I'm sure they'll sell immediately.

"Yes. Yes," Abby exclaims. "This is better than roses. It's beautiful." She claps her hands excitedly.

Inspiration hits, and when the girls leave, I make wonderful displays for the front window. Willow drops in for a while and brings us coffees. Charli comes in to check on her brother and remind him he has homework to finish. She ends up calling a bride she's designing a dress for and referring her to me for her wedding day flowers.

I'm so busy that I don't realize how fast the time has flown by. When I lift my head from the last bunch of flowers, it's dark outside. Thunder is sending Noah home when the headlights of an Escalade start rolling by slowly in front of the shop. It doesn't come to a stop, but the passenger door is thrown open and a body flies out and rolls to the curb.

I screech in horror, covering my mouth with my hands. Noah's about to run out the door, but Thunder yanks him back inside.

"You wait here," he says.

As Thunder's about to step outside, I grasp his hand. "Don't go," I beg.

"I'm not alone." He jerks his head to the door, where Saint and Hammer are sprinting across the street. I let him go and watch as he runs out to meet the others. Saint crouches over the body, raking his hand through his hair, then across his face. I can see the anguish in his face. Whoever it is, they're dead.

Thunder and Hammer are down on their haunches next to him. They slowly stand up, huddled together. Thunder looks back at Noah and me, shaking his head. Noah pulls me away from the door and farther into the room and guides me to a chair. He hands me a glass of water, keeping a soothing hand on my shoulder.

I hear sirens and cars pulling up to the shop with their lights flashing. The police have arrived. I wait for Thunder to come back to me, I'm thinking things just got worse.

Thunder

Guard stands by my side as the cops ask their questions. We used to have a rough relationship with the sheriff and his men, then they finally saw what the Pride was all about, and they relented. Recently, we've even worked together on several occasions, mostly when a skip happens and they call Ghost to find the guy, but we've all come to an understanding, respecting each other's boundaries.

The girl was dead before she hit the ground, beaten to shit, then a bullet to the heart. The person who did this is sending a message. A bloody message meant to rattle Rose.

Whoever this woman is, she has track marks down her arms. A junkie. Her revealing clothing suggests she worked the streets. Saint did a quick assessment of her before the sheriff arrived and confirmed our assumption. They beat her bloody, but why? And who the hell is she?

No purse or ID. Nothing to tell us who she is, which means we need to wait for forensics to do their thing, then have Orion hack into their records to find out. It could be that it doesn't matter who she is, but the message they're sending is clearly to obey, or else.

Sofia was called to the scene immediately. Guard takes no chances when a body is dropped off practically at our doorstep. Doesn't happen often, but we know how to ensure our protection. We have our little pit bull to protect our interests. I think even the sheriff is intimidated by Sofia's intelligence.

"Go to Rose," Guard says. "We've got this, and she needs you." The brothers have rallied, and when I scan the street, I see them all. Demon is front and center, but Steady, War, Orion, Risk, and the others are all here too.

"Yeah." I let out a heavy breath. "This is going to fuck

with her head. The phone call earlier was a warning. This fucker is upping his game to screw with her."

Risk steps forward. "I'll call Reno. I'll update him and see if he's heard anything yet."

"I took a photo of her face. See if he or anyone can ID the girl," Saint adds. I didn't even think of doing that. Jesus! Normally, I would be right on that.

Guard senses what I'm thinking. "Knock it off. Your first and most important task is looking out for your woman. You did the right thing."

"What do you think this means?" I ask. I know that Guard has this uncanny ability to feel and sense danger and predict what comes next. It used to freak me out, but now I see the possibilities of this gift.

"This blood-soaked, messy message is meant to tell the Pride to get out of the way of what they want. That's not going to happen. They want a war, they'll get one," he declares. Ghost is right beside his brother, and he and Guard exchange glances.

"Is it going to come to that?" Ghost asks, but I think he already knows the answer.

"You kill a woman and dump her body in our territory, you have to understand you're overstepping your bounds. What do you think?" Guard retorts with fury in his tone.

"Fuck!" Ghost grumbles. He looks at the shop, then to me. It's time to take care of my girl.

TWELVE

That Was Easy

THUNDER

Noah hasn't left Rosie's side. He's a good kid and is proving himself to be a loyal Pride member. He's too young to join, and we're respecting Charli's wishes to have him go to school before he makes up his mind whether the club is for him or not. Either way, he's always going to be part of us because Wildcard and Charli belong to us, so that makes Noah a part of us as well.

Rosie jumps up from her chair and comes to me.

"Who—who was it?" She gulps.

"A young woman." I keep my tone calm and low.

"She—she's dead, isn't she?"

I nod. Her shoulders slump and she lets out a heavy, ragged sigh. "She was a junkie. We're going to find out who she is."

"She died from an overdose?" Fuck! I hate to do this to Rosie, but she needs to know the truth.

"No, baby." I let my fingers touch the soft strands of her dark hair, looking into her chocolate-brown eyes, knowing what I tell her next is going to hurt her deeply. "She was beaten. Pretty badly."

"Oh my God! Who are these people?" she says in a harsh whisper. She rests her head on my chest. "This is too much. Too damn much." She lets out a ragged breath. "They tossed her away like garbage. Right in front of my store."

I wrap my arms around her; she reciprocates, clasping my jacket. "It's going to be all right," I murmur. "I promise." I want to keep her in my arms, but the shrill ring of the telephone breaks us apart. I don't give her the chance to pick up and do it myself, not wanting her to have to deal with anything else tonight. "Hello?"

"Uh, hello? I think I may have the wrong number. I'm looking for Petals, the flower shop," Penny's unsure voice says.

"Penny?"

"Who is this? Is Rose there?"

"Yeah, let me get her for you." I pass the receiver to Rosie.

"Hi, Mom." After a brief pause, Rosie says, "It's Michael." A pause. "That's right. Michael Donally." After another pause, she adds, "He lives in town. Michael walked into my shop to pick up some flowers, and we got to talking." Rosie looks at her shoes and shuffles from foot to foot. "We're seeing each other, Mom."

I can't help but chuckle. She glares at me angrily, and I can hear her mother talking a mile a minute, although I can't make out what she's saying. That is until I hear her call for her husband.

"Hi, Dad. Yes, it's true," she says quietly. "I like him. A lot." Rosie brightens up, a smile on her lips as she listens to her father on the other end. "He's right beside me." Another short pause before she says, "I'll talk to you soon.

Love you." Then the minx holds the phone out to me. "Dad wants to say hello."

"Hello, Erik." Erik has been a supportive and caring father. I admired the way he stood by his girls. He's a family man. His wife is his queen and his daughters his princesses. The devastation that hit their family when Clarissa went off the rails knocked Erik on his ass. We sat in his garage for hours talking about the next steps for Clarissa's recovery. He treated me like his own kid, offering support and guidance.

The night I walked away from Clarissa, I walked away from Erik and his family too. I expect to get an earful, and perhaps it's warranted from his perspective. I brace myself for the worst.

"It's been a long time, son," Erik says calmly.

"It really has. I'm sorry for—"

"None of that," he cuts in. "There was nothing you could do. And I've finally come to accept there was nothing I could do. Change only happens when you want it. My Clarry had to fly free and wild. Her purpose was her own. Her story wasn't always pretty, but there were moments of glorious sunshine that I hold on to. You did what you had to do to distance yourself, son. It would have eaten at you. But Rosie tells me that you're seeing one another. That true?"

"It is."

I can hear footsteps as he walks, then a door shuts. "I always knew there was something between you and Rose. More than a big brother watching out for her. You're a man who's going to do what you need to do, but I'm going to ask you to tread carefully. She's spunky and funny and will make you think she's tough as nails, but my little girl has a soft underbelly."

"Erik, you should see her place. It's filled with pink and

glitter," I reply, only to hear him laugh. "I feel like unicorns and fairies are going to follow us home." He laughs even louder. "But I hear you and am taking care." I take a breath, then lay my cards on the table. "I know who Rose is. There's no comparison, and I care about her because she is Rose." I want to make it perfectly clear that this isn't about finding a part of Clarissa. This is seeing Rosie for who she is and loving her for what she has become.

"I understand. Rose walked in the shadow of her older sister for a long time. It took a while for her to come into her own, and when she did, she did it big. Big dreams, full of independence, and she always knew what she wanted. Treat my girl right," he says.

"That I can promise you." We chat for a few more minutes about his retirement and how they've settled into their new space. Erik loves to golf and is on the course a couple of times a week, while Penny is volunteering at the local hospital. Erik never mentions anything suspicious, and I take that as a good sign that no one is nosing around them.

When I hang up, Rosie is right beside me. "That sounded like it went well," she says hopefully.

I reach out to touch her cheek. "Your father's a good man, babe. He wants you to be happy, and I'm going to do my damn best to give you that." I wrap my arm around her shoulders. The events of the evening have been intense. "Are you doing okay?"

Rosie releases a heavy sigh. "I'm fine, right now. Noah is a great comfort." She looks over to where Noah is situated across the room. "He didn't leave me for a second."

"He's a good kid." I turn my attention in his direction. "Yo, Noah, we'll drop you off at Charli and Wildcard's place."

"I'm supposed to stay at the club tonight," he says.

"Not tonight. Charli's going to want you home."

Noah nods. We both know Charli, and when shit like this goes down, having Noah home makes her feel better. Charli's been looking after Noah for years, and after Noah fell in with a nasty crowd, she's been overprotective. Noah's free and clear from those guys, but the wound is still fresh, and since Charli's the only family Noah has, she's responsible for her brother. I tell Rose, "We're staying at the club tonight."

"What? Why?"

"I'm meeting with the brothers, and it'll get late. We'll go to your place first, and you can pack an overnight bag. I have my own room. It's comfortable, and the place is a fortress."

She doesn't put up a fight. She's probably emotionally exhausted. Rosie looks tired. She worked like a madwoman getting the shop ready, and then this happens. She needs food and sleep.

I, on the other hand, need answers. This shit needs to end. I want to know who the fuck is responsible for wreaking havoc in Rosie's life and our club. Then I want to find the bastard and rip his dick off and shove it down his throat.

I know how to contain my anger. I've trained myself from an early age to control my temper, and that's just what I'm doing for Rosie's sake. She doesn't need to see me lose it. It's not easy to watch people you love walk away from you. My parents emotionally left me, and it hurt. I battled that war within myself and decided that I get to choose how I react. It was a simple decision after that. They weren't going to have that power over me.

Rosie and I get to the compound, and even though I want to get to Orion to see what he's found out, I take my time getting Rosie settled. Dinner is sandwiches and chips, but she doesn't seem to care. Her eyes are practically closing while she eats.

My room is up the stairs, at the very end of the hall. It's one of the bigger rooms, with its own bathroom. This has been my home, my quiet place. Yet tonight when I walk in, it doesn't have the same warm feeling I got from Rosie's home.

Rosie is ready to drop. I sit with my back against the headboard as she settles in my bed. I stroke her soft hair and listen to her soft sighs before she falls asleep. Apart from the progress of the shop being ready to open tomorrow, it's been a crazy day. I wasn't sure how Erik was going to react when Rosie told him about us. I guess I was expecting outrage, but Erik made it easy.

We had a close relationship until I took off. Erik didn't need an explanation and didn't want one. He knew I had to get away. He didn't blame me; he took that on himself. I'm glad he's come to terms with who was really responsible: Clarissa herself.

Easy is waking up in the morning and watching Rose sip coffee, smiling. Easy is unloading a truckful of boxes and knowing it makes her happy. Easy is acceptance of who I am to Rosie and letting me be part of Erik and Penny's family. I like easy.

THIRTEEN

Face the Day

THUNDER

I drag myself away from Rosie, leaving her curled up in my bed, and head back down the stairs. Orion is in the office we've set up with every possible gadget a computer guy would want. Orion's the best there is. The only one comparable is Dante Viale. He's Reno's younger brother, and between the two of them, I'm hoping we'll find the connection between the dead woman and the bastard terrorizing Rose.

Guard and Ghost are already there, along with Saint and Risk.

"Is Rose all right?" Saint asks as soon as he sees me.

"Shaken up, for sure, but she's hanging in there."

"Yeah, well, it ain't every day a body goes flying out of a car directly in front of your store," Risk says. "She's tougher than she looks." I have to agree with him. Anyone else would have crumbled by now.

Orion looks up from his screen. "I did a reconstruction of the woman's face, and I'm running it through a recognition program. It may take a while. The morgue has Jane

Doe slotted for autopsy tomorrow morning. I'll be checking periodically for the final report."

"She died from a gunshot to the heart. What's curious is that she was beaten first," Saint says. "If she was an out-of-line whore, why bother beating her if you were going to kill her anyway? And why kill her at all if she was making you money? A pimp's goal is to use these women for cash. Why kill your revenue stream?"

"She could have been causing drama," Guard adds.

"Then you slap her around and set her straight," Ghost responds, shaking his head.

I'm inclined to agree with him on that. "Nah, there's a connection. A message. They dumped her in front of Rose's shop. It's a message for her."

Orion says, "Thunder's right. We need to get a handle on who's pulling the strings. I get the idea that the pimp, Harvey, was taking orders from someone higher up. Once we know who he is, then we'll have a trail of breadcrumbs to follow."

There's a dinging sound from the computer, and a face flashes onto the screen. Pretty blonde-haired girl about sixteen or seventeen years old. Looks like she belongs in the cornfields of Iowa, all fresh-faced and smiling.

"Cora Davis went missing five years ago. Parents reported her disappearance. Police deemed her a runaway," Orion says. He types rapidly into the keyboard and pulls up the information from her file. "Parents insist she was kidnapped. They're offering their own reward for any information about their daughter and her safe return. They most recently petitioned to have the case reopened with a witness who said they saw their daughter in the city. The request was denied."

"It could be the woman from today," Ghost murmurs. The woman was so badly beaten that the best form of identification would be fingerprints and dental records, and they won't be available to us until tomorrow. All we have to work with are the photos taken at the time, and Orion's facial reconstruction software. It's a good program, but with the damage to the woman's face, we're working with our best guess.

"She may have run away and gotten into trouble. Young pretty girl, looking to start a life on her own in the big city. It happens all the time," Saint points out.

"Or a nice girl is lured into becoming a prostitute and they keep her in line by drugging her and turning her into an addict," Guard counters.

"Either way, the story sucks," I tell them. "We can't even confirm it's her. It could be, but may not be."

"My gut says it's the same person," Guard says. "Let's find out all we can about her parents, school, friends. Let's see if we have any club close by that can dig up information on her life before her disappearance," he tells Orion.

"On it," he responds.

"For now, we wait, and reconvene once Orion gets a positive ID. Then we decide our next move. Everyone, get some sleep," Guard orders as he makes his way to the door. He looks over his shoulder. "Our women don't go out alone."

"Do they ever?" Ghost says.

"No, but if these guys are watching, they know Rose has built friendships with our old ladies. When they're not at work, they're here. I'm moving Ava to the compound in the morning. We'll be tight, but we can make it work," he says.

If Guard is bringing his woman here, that means he feels the severity of the situation. The rest of the men will follow suit. The compound was built for safety. It was designed to house the men and their families. Our families have grown exponentially, and I think we're going to have to add on. We'll make do with what we've got. Guard's right, though. It's easier to keep watch if we're all in one place and less taxing on our resources. I'm not sure how Rosie will react, but that's a problem for tomorrow.

Rose

T*he next morning…*

I didn't even hear Thunder come to bed last night, I was so exhausted. I want to wake him, but he looks so peaceful. And hot! He's lying on his back with a hand slung over his head, his bare chest on display and the sheet hanging low around his hips. His vibrant tattoos are on display. I read the words *I choose…* in bold letters etched in black ink on his ribs, with a date underneath. He told me that the date represents that day he left home and decided to be the master of his destiny. It's beautiful. He's beautiful. His hair is loose, out of his normal man bun, in messy disarray over the pillow, and I itch to touch his chiseled body.

And so I do. I run my fingertips over the edge of his tattoo, feeling the hardness of his chest beneath the silk of his skin. A touch doesn't seem like enough. I press my lips on his shoulder, barely a touch, but enough to make me want more.

Thunder's arm tightens around me. "Don't stop now, Rosie. I like it," he murmurs in a sleepy haze, with a sexy smile that makes my toes curl. I become bolder, sliding my hand down his body to the edge of the sheet, finding his hard cock proudly erect and waiting for me. I take him in my hand, feeling the contours of his manhood, then slide my hand up and down, stroking him.

A rough sensual growl from my man tells me I'm doing it just as he likes it. I hold him tighter and quicken my pace, thoroughly enjoying myself as I watch Thunder's desire grow. His moans only spur me on.

"I want your mouth, baby," he murmurs huskily, making me quiver inside. I crawl between his legs as he moves farther up the headboard. Before I can make my move, his hands come under my pajama tee, and he whips it off, tossing it to the side. "I want you naked." He motions with a jerk of his head to my tiny shorts. "Off," he orders.

Is it possible to come just from his words? Because I swear I felt a tingle rush through me, and my panties are soaked. I wriggle out of my shorts and panties. His fingers graze over the tips of my nipples, making them as hard as pebbles under his touch. "Whatcha going to do to me?" he asks with a grin.

I close my mouth over the tip of his cock, eliciting a primitive, guttural moan. I circle my tongue around and around, then slide it gently through his very sensitive slit, tasting a salty drop of his essence. He reaches out, pulling my hair off my face so he can watch me suck him off. I bob my head up and down. Not an easy feat seeing as he's a large man and his member follows suit. I let my hands slide down between his legs, cupping his balls, softly massaging them. The muscles in his thighs tense, and suddenly, he pulls his cock out of my mouth.

Within seconds, I'm shifted, completely turned about, with my ass to his face. "Now, continue," he says, and before I can do a single thing, his hands tighten on my hips, pulling me downward onto his mouth. He starts eating my pussy.

"Oh my God!" I moan, loving the feel of his tongue in

my pussy. He slaps my ass as a reminder that I have work to do. I take him back into my mouth and suck and lick him as voraciously as he does me. I moan around his cock, only spurring him closer to his release as he does with mine. When he plunges two fingers inside me, I can't hold off anymore. My orgasm rips through me, racking through my body. I take my man deeper in my mouth, wanting him to feel the same euphoria, and within seconds, I'm rewarded, swallowing down every succulent drop of him.

Thunder moves me to lie over him, taking my mouth in a passionate kiss. His hands hold my head steady as he ravages my mouth, until our breaths are labored. When he wrenches his lips from mine, he stares into my eyes.

"I love you, Rose. God help me, I think I have for years and years." His eyes are soft and warm, full of love.

"I loved you from the first moment I saw you. I wanted you to be mine. I've never forgotten you. I used to dream that we would find one another someday. A silly dream I would tell myself. Then one day, there you were, just as magnificent as I remembered you. And what's more, you want me. *Me.*" I shake my head unbelievingly. "Sometimes, I'm afraid this is just a dream."

He pulls me in for another earth-shattering kiss. "No dream. This is us."

This is the moment I'll remember for the rest of my life. If I could, I'd keep us just as we are, in this room, and forget the rest of the world exists. This is joy. This is happiness.

Unfortunately, a loud rap on the door tells us that we're not alone, and eventually, we're going to need to get out of bed and face the day.

FOURTEEN

Best Part of the Day

ROSE

It's surprising to see Ava and Vi downstairs in the kitchen making breakfast. Vi is flipping pancakes while Ava's tending to the bacon and eggs. Both seem engrossed in their tasks and don't notice Thunder or me come in.

"Hey," I greet them, and they both turn to me.

"Hello, sunshine," Vi exclaims. "Give us a hand, will you?"

"Put me to work," I say.

With a giggle, Ava hands me a loaf of bread. "Toast with butter. And don't skimp on the butter." She rolls her eyes. "The men like their butter."

I'm getting to work on the toast when Hanna and Abigail walk in. They immediately take out plates and cutlery, carrying it to the other room, where Hanna tells us the boys are setting up tables for us all to sit.

It's not until more of the Lady Pride arrive that I start to wonder if something's up. Everyone is bustling around, doing their part, and everybody seems happy enough, but a large gathering midweek seems a little strange.

Once we're all sitting around the table and I'm next to Thunder, I know something's up. Orion looks at his phone and leaves the table, only to come back for Guard. Guard quietly follows, and both are gone for quite some time. I turn to Thunder and see that Guard's actions haven't gone unnoticed. His gaze follows the other guys, but everyone remains silent, their exchanged glances speaking for them.

"What's going on?" I whisper to Thunder.

"Not sure yet. We'll find out soon enough."

"I need to get to the shop. Can you drive me in?" I ask. Thunder took me in yesterday, and I never considered driving my car over last night.

"We've got time. You don't open for another hour," he says.

"I like to be there early."

"We'll get you there."

Guard calls out for Thunder and adds, "Bring Rose with you." I scan the table as I get up. I can see the worried expressions, although Ava does give my hand a squeeze and a tight smile.

With Orion and Guard sitting on the sofa in his office, we join them in the chairs across from them. "I'm not sure how much Thunder's told you," Guard starts.

"Nothing," Thunder says. "I wanted to wait until we had more information."

"We have positive identification that the woman is the same girl reported missing five years ago, Cora Davis. She also worked for John Harvey. The same pimp your sister was hooked up with," Orion says.

"Harvey seems to be the link," Guard says. "He's dead, but someone has taken over his business, and they're collecting on old debts. Demon is already on it. So is Dante from the Viale clan. The body dump was a message, Rose. These guys aren't fucking around."

"But I don't even know them. After my sister left, she had nothing to do with us." My voice trembles. My nerves are shattered.

"We got that." Guard's tone softens. "But these people are ruthless. We're hoping we can find out who's calling the shots and have a sit-down with them. It may take a few days or a few weeks, but we're aiming for sooner rather than later. In the meantime, we're all staying at the compound. It's the most secure place, and it'll be easier for us to keep watch on one place than several."

It finally dawns on me. "That's why everyone's here!"

"Yeah, babe. I wanted to tell you this morning," Thunder says, wrapping an arm around my shoulders. "That means you're either at work or at the club. We'll go by your place, and we'll pack more of your stuff."

"But if I stay here, you're all in danger," I say, horrified. Oh my God, what have I brought to their doorstep? "Maybe, I'd better—"

"Don't fucking say it, Rosie." Thunder raises his voice, making me jump.

Guard gives him a stern look. "Calm down. Rose isn't going anywhere, and neither are you." Then he turns to me. "I know you're scared, but this the safest place for you. What we're doing is precautionary. This isn't the first time, nor will it be the last, that we pull our families together. The women know the routine. The kids love being together. They always have a blast."

"My parents—"

"We've got another club helping out. Good men. Smart men. They're keeping watch. So far, no one has approached them," Guard says soothingly.

"I know it's hard since you don't know us well, but you've got to let us do our thing," Orion says.

"I trust you," I say, looking him straight in the eye. Then I move my gaze to Guard. "I trust you all."

Orion grins, and Guard gives me a huge smile. "You're part of the Pride, Rose. Easy as that."

"None of this is easy. To tell you the truth, all this is making me sick. I left to go out on my own and see what I can accomplish, and this black cloud is looming over me and sucking you into the storm. I don't want any of this for you. Any of you!" I say, looking at the three men and settling my gaze on Thunder.

"One day soon, this is going to be a story we tell our kids. Cheer up, Rosie. The sun is going to shine real soon," Thunder says, pulling me in close and placing a chaste kiss on my forehead. "Now, I'll take you to work. I'm with you for the day."

"What about your own work?"

"We're covering for him," Orion replies.

"You're to tell us when you're heading out. I want another man with you," Guard insists, looking directly at Thunder.

"I'm sorry I'm causing so much trouble," I tell Guard.

"You're no trouble." He shakes his head. "People selling drugs to kids, making them into prostitutes, using them, and abusing them, that's the trouble. We can't stop all the ugliness of the world, but this is our town, and we don't allow that shit here."

With that, Thunder and I take our leave. I help clear the dishes from the table before we head for the shop. Ava gives me a big hug before I walk out and whispers in my ear, "We've got your back."

Thunder

It's good that the shop has been missed and customers are coming through. Some come to say hello to Rosie and have a chat, but end up leaving with a purchase in hand. Others like to browse, looking for that special gift. Rose takes her time with each person. She listens, giving them ideas that might work. Rosie has always been good with people. Young or old, she seems to find common ground and sets them at ease.

The few days of having to close was a hit to her bank account, but today has been busy, and if this is any indication of her future for the shop, she's going to do well. With a couple of hours left in the day, things begin to slow down, and she gets to tidying up. I'm mostly in the back, moving boxes and organizing her small storage space to make it easier for her to move around. Petals is her baby, and I want her to know I support her.

The chiming of the bell over the door grabs my attention. I come out of the back to see a man with his son. I've seen this guy around. He's a truck driver and used to work for a trucking company that recently went out of business. He looks haggard, but he has a hand on his son's shoulder, who stands proudly beside him.

"How can I help you lovely gentlemen?" Rosie asks.

The father looks down on his son, nodding. "Go ahead, Robbie." The kid's the spitting image of his father, with straight sandy-brown hair and hazel eyes. They even have the same stance, standing tall and proud.

Robbie opens the palm of his hand. I can see the crushed bills. "Is this enough to buy my mom a rose? It's her birthday. She loves flowers."

Rose moves down to his level and gently takes his hand in hers, studying the money. From where I am, I can see that the kid doesn't have enough to cover the cost.

"You're in luck!" she declares. "We're having a special today. You can buy three roses with that." The boy lights up like he been given a shiny new bike to ride. He looks up at his father. The guy knows Rose is lying and I can see he's conflicted in setting his son straight or letting him have this for his mother.

"Hey." I step forward. I offer my hand to the guy. "Name's Thunder."

"Robert Kelpner." He shakes my hand.

"I've seen you around. You drive a rig, right?" I already know he does, but I want to see his reaction. He straightens taller and meets my eyes, a glint of hope shining through.

"Yes, I do. I used to work for Dolman's Trucking, but they went out of business six months ago. I've been doing long hauls as I can get them." Long hauls suck. That means more time away from the family and more stress.

"Not sure if you're interested. I got a buddy in the next town over looking for a daily delivery guy. Car and motorcycle parts, mainly, but supplies as well. The company is growing and needs to add on new routes. You interested?"

"Well, yeah. Absolutely," he says.

"You know the parts store across the way here in town? Go tomorrow morning and ask for War. He'll get you in touch with they guy. They're close friends. Don't let the big man scare you. He's a great guy. I'll let him know you're coming," I say. Wanting to be fully upfront, I tell him, "It's a Pride business. We're legit and we do right by our employees, but I want you to have all the facts."

"I've got no problem with that. I hear what you've done for this town and the work that's come because of it," Robert says, his face beaming with a smile. He looks at the counter, where Rosie has lured Robbie to help pick out the colors for his mom's flowers.

"He seems like a good kid," I say.

"He's the best kid. Smart and looks after his mom when I'm away. It's not right that he has to grow up that fast." He sighs. "He's using his savings to buy those for her. Marnie's pregnant with our second, and things are tight with the baby coming and all," he confesses.

"Go see War. Then go to the clinic and talk to Saint. Like I said, we take care of our employees. You treat us right, we treat you right," I tell him.

"Saint?"

"The clinic in town, he's one of ours. Your wife needs a doctor close by, and he's the best."

"All ready, Dad. Aren't these great?" Robbie is proudly holding a bouquet with three pink roses and baby's breath. "Mom's going to be so surprised."

"Thank you." Two simple words that hold a lot of meaning.

L*ater that night…*

With the group safely at the compound, I leave Rosie in good hands with Maddie and Izzy while I go talk to War about the visit he's going to get from Robert tomorrow. I explain the situation while Orion runs a background check to make sure he is who he says. We can't be too careful, and Guard's rules are there for a reason.

Orion rambles off what he's found. "Guy's clean. A couple of parking tickets in all his driving days. No accidents, and he was the last one let go from his last job. His boss liked him and respected him. He's accumulating debt since being let go, but he makes the minimum payments at the very least."

"Right. We need a good man, and if this works out, it's a win, win, for everyone," War replies.

I shift our talk to the bigger issue. "Got anything new on Cora? Or the new game in town that killed her boss?"

Orion says, "Demon's people are working on it. All he's got so far is that Clarissa and Cora both worked for Harvey. The other women in his harem looked for protection elsewhere as soon as Harvey was killed. Demon thinks he's found a woman who can give him more information, but she's not talking. He says she's scared to death and refuses to even meet with him."

"It hasn't been confirmed, but the new player is Russian with ties to the mob," Guard says as he walks through the door. "Demon will find a way to get to the girl," he adds. "Spoke with Dante and he's checking out the situation and takeover of Harvey's territory. He's not convinced it's the Russians."

"This sit-and-wait game is killing me," I grumble.

"Patience has never been your strong suit." Guard laughs, clapping a hand on my shoulder. "We're getting closer. Enjoy the evening with Rose. Tomorrow is another day."

"The best part of the day was that kid," I say. Guard knows my history and my lack of a relationship with my parents. "He was so happy carrying those flowers out the door."

"Kids are pure and honest. It's a shame that the world has a way of tainting them as they get older. His parents have given him the love he needs, and that's a hell of a lot more powerful than any amount of money," Guard states. Truer words were never spoken. I would have given up every gadget I had to have a real relationship with my parents. "You did a good thing today. You gave the guy hope. Hope for his family and for the future."

FIFTEEN

Talk or Fight

THUNDER

After the talk with Guard and the others, I go looking for Rosie. Maddie tells me she went upstairs to our room. As I come through the door, I hear the shower running and Rosie singing. I push the bathroom door open a crack and see her silhouette through the steamed glass.

She looks like a goddess with her head tipped back, water streaming down over her hourglass shape. Her long brown silky hair cascades down her back, her eyes are closed, and her hands are running over her body.

It's a sight too tempting to ignore. I undress quickly and slide open the shower stall. Her head whips around as she clasps a hand to her chest.

"You scared the life out of me," she breathes.

"I'll make it up to you," I say, stepping inside. It's not a large space, and when Rose steps back to accommodate my large frame, she's up against the tiled wall. I place my hands on either side of her head, lowering my mouth to hers. Electricity surges between us. It happens every time our lips touch.

Without delay, her arms come around my neck, and I press my body into hers, wanting to feel her bare skin against mine. Our kiss is fevered and hot. I can't get enough of her. Her fingers dig into my scalp, holding me to her. Little mewls of desire escape from her lips and she wriggles, lifting a leg and hitching it around mine. She grinds her lower half against me.

"Does my girl need more?" I tease.

"Yes. I need you," she moans, pulling my head back down to nip at my lower lip.

I lift her up, and her legs come around my waist. "I'll always give you what you need," I tell her, then kiss her long and sweet as I thrust inside her wet and waiting pussy. Our lovemaking isn't soft. It's desperate, clingy, hard, and fast. Her nails dig into my shoulders, marking me as her own.

Her head tilts back as she comes undone in my arms. Her body shudders as her orgasm tears through her. Her eyes grow wide, and she calls out my name. I'm so close to my own release. I feel her teeth graze my lobe.

"I love you, baby," she whispers.

I come hard, thrusting once and again until I root myself deep inside my woman and let myself go with a roar. It takes a couple of minutes before I can set her on her feet. With the cloth in hand, I lather it and run it over her body, carefully, ensuring I'm gentle when I clean between her legs.

Rosie watches me with wide-eyed innocence, letting me look after her. I wash up quicky, then turn off the water, lead her out, and wrap a towel around her.

"Don't bother getting dressed. I'm hungry for my woman's pussy. Go get ready for me, baby. On my bed, legs spread wide. Will you do that for me?" I move a strand of hair out of her eyes and tuck it around her ear.

With a pink tinge to her cheeks, Rosie gives me a shy grin as she nods and scampers out. It never ceases to amaze me how shy she can still get. I touched, licked, and fucked her, and I can't get enough of her. Even my cock, which was just milked dry, is ready to go again.

As I come into the bedroom, there she is, waiting for me, just as I asked. I climb in from the bottom of the bed, running the tips of my fingers up and down the inside of her thighs, taking in the pretty pink pussy waiting for me to devour it with my tongue.

I don't disappoint her. I eat her delicious core and suck her clit until she's hoarse from screaming, making her come twice more before giving her my cock again, taking us both over the edge.

"We can't go back down," she exclaims a while later, then her voice becomes a loud whisper. "They might have heard me. I'll never be able to show my face again." Rosie covers her face with her hands as I tug away the sheets from around her.

"Baby, no one will care," I say. I really want to chuckle, but I don't think Rosie would appreciate it. The guys in the club fuck often and hard. I've heard their women time and time again. They sure as hell don't care. I try to placate her. "We're at the farthest end of the building. I'm sure your voice didn't carry that far." I know for sure it sure as hell did, but no way in hell am I telling her that.

"Can't we stay here?" She pouts.

"We need food. That's down there." I point to the door.

"I'm not hungry. You go." She's a terrible liar, and her stomach betrays her as it rumbles its own frustration.

"Not hungry, huh?" I lean forward, bracing my fists on the bed, caging her in. "These are our people, our family, and even if they did hear you, which I'm sure they didn't, they'd never embarrass you."

"Oh, okay," she relents, blowing out a breath. She shimmies out from under the sheets and begins to dress. As she puts on her panties, her perfectly rounded derriere is the ultimate view. I'm thinking that we could do without sustenance. The tight-fitting jeans emphasize every luscious curve, and the tank top shows off her toned arms and shoulders. She pulls her damp hair up into a messy bun and turns to face me. "One snicker and I'm leaving," she warns.

"One snicker and I'll punch them in the mouth so they won't be able to smile for a month." I grin.

As we head down, Rosie hesitates on the last step, but finally joins the others. Not a word is said, and Hanna rounds Rose up to help set the table. Roscoe and I grab extra chairs, arranging them around the table. The other men are getting the kids to the table.

Gavin, Guard's oldest son, is the oldest of the new generation of Pride men. If Gavin is half the man his father is, he'll be a fantastic leader and president. His brother Ryder is a rabble-rouser, quick and clever, but he needs a guiding hand to keep him on track. Both boys are great kids, just like the others. I see Romeo being the thinker of the group. He's watchful and sees everything. Dean and Alexander are too young for me to make an assessment, but I notice them wanting to be part of the boys' group. Dean toddles over and sits himself right in the middle of it all, and Alexander follows.

This doesn't mean the little princesses of the Pride don't get a whole lot of attention. Gabby, our little fashion-ista, is a mini Vi, full of personality and fun loving. Amelia is very quiet, but Gabby brings her out of her shell. Together, they're going to drive the boys crazy, along with their fathers.

Amelia tugs on Rosie's hand, wanting her to sit next to her at the table. Amelia whispers something in her ear and giggles. Rosie returns the favor until they're both laughing.

When we all come to the table, I lean in and ask, "Sharing secrets?"

Rosie looks over at Amelia, then slides her eyes back to me. "Girl talk. You're not a girl, and we can't tell."

Amelia smiles so big, her rosy cheeks and bright smile light up the room. "Does Mama get to know your secret?" Maddie asks, leaning in and kissing the little girl's cheek.

"I'll tell you at bedtime," Amelia whispers loudly, putting her forefinger to her lips to shush her mom.

"That's some special secret if you can't tell your Uncle Thunder," I tease.

"It's a happy one," she exclaims. The softhearted tyke suddenly feels that she should share and climbs down from her chair and into my lap. Her small hands cup my ear, and she says, "I like Rosie. I want you to marry her."

I give Amelia a big snuggle. "I think that's a wonderful idea when the time is right," I murmur in her ear.

"When is that?"

"I'll let you know, sunshine." Amelia is satisfied with that. She gives me another hug before going back to her chair.

They say "out of the mouths of babes," and it's true. Children see things so plainly. Someone makes you happy, so you make them part of your life forever to keep that happiness going. It's when I think of how the world will test that innocence that makes me angry.

I scan Rose's profile. She must sense it and turns to me. "What is it?" she asks.

I lift her hand to my lips and kiss her fingers. "I'm happy, baby."

She leans in and brushes her lips over mine. "Me too."

Rose

With the kids all tucked in, the guys settle in to either play pool or watch the game. In pairs, they take turns walking the perimeter of the clubhouse, making sure that everything is as it should be. Orion and Vi head to the IT room, where he keeps an eye on the security system.

"Is it always like this?" I ask Ava.

She tilts her head. "What do you mean?"

"The security and stuff."

"Not always, but Guard believes in taking safety measures. There's a lot you don't know about my man, but this is one thing you can count on: his life is devoted to his family and this club. We're his to protect. That's how he got his road name, Guard."

"Thunder said he got his name because he strikes like a thunderstorm. Fast and turbulent."

"Yeah. They all have a reason for their road names. The club picks it for them when they get their patch." She points out Priest. "Priest because he keeps it all in. Whatever you tell him stays with him until you're ready to share." She tips her head to Wildcard. "That one can go either way. Fury or calm, but always loyal." Her eyes move to Hammer. "He was nicknamed Hammer in the military. It seems to suit him, since he hits hard and fights harder. It's also a testament to the men he served with. Most of these guys served our country. Ghost lost his whole unit.

He was the only one who survived. That takes a toll on a man."

"Poor Ghost." Sadness washes over me.

"He's home now and has the love of his life by his side, healing his wounds. He has his brothers and all of us," Ava says.

It's not until Risk and Saint rush through the door and shout, "We got company, and this isn't good," that we all jump to our feet.

"Everyone, load up and take your positions," Guard shouts. He looks at Ava. "Quick as you can, get the kids and the women into the back room. Shut that door. It doesn't open until I come for you," he orders. He pulls Noah by the arm. "You go with them. I need to know they're safe."

Everyone's running around, but I'm frozen to my spot. Thunder gives me a little shake. "Don't lose it on me now, Rosie. Go with the others." I'm still too stunned to speak or move. Charli grabs my hand and drags me after her while I glance over at Thunder and wonder what the hell is happening.

"Are they coming to talk or fight?" I hear Thunder ask.

"Either way, no one gets in here," Saint replies.

That's the last thing I hear or see before being closed in a room with a steel door with the other women and their children. Most of the kids are sleeping in their mothers' arms. I glance around the room to see cots, blankets, canned food, and all you would need for Armageddon. The mothers put their kids down and lull them to sleep. The others help where they can. Charli is continuing to hold my hand tightly. Noah stands firmly at the door, just as he was told.

"This is all because of me," I murmur, guilt and panic welling in my heart. "I brought this to you. All of you." I begin to shake uncontrollably. Charli calls out for Camille, who rushes over with a blanket. She wraps it around my shoulders and guides me to sit on a chair.

"She's going into shock. Get her some water," Camille says. She grips my chin, her eyes meeting mine. "Breathe with me," she says. I follow her breathing, inhaling, exhaling.

Eventually, I'm able to regain my composure. "What if someone gets hurt?"

Vi answers, "Someone will, but it won't be Satan's Pride."

SIXTEEN

The Meeting

THUNDER

"Shake it off, man! Best thing you can do for her is concentrate on keeping her safe," Saint tells me as he hands me a gun from the rack we have concealed in the back panel walls, hidden behind the bookshelves.

I know he's right and pull myself together. I grip the weapon and take my place next to Guard and Orion. Normally, I'd be posted out of sight, but they've come for Rose, and that puts me at the front of the line.

A black Lincoln Continental comes rolling up to the iron gate of the compound. The electric fence runs along the entire perimeter of our property. We've even added a few traps along the way that Wildcard has activated. He's sitting at the security camera watching every move and ready to initiate action if necessary.

The driver opens his door and comes around to the passenger side. An older man emerges from the car, white hair with receding hairline and a potbelly, dressed in a dark blue, exceptionally well-tailored suit. He takes a step forward, flanked by two of his men.

It hasn't gone unnoticed that several other cars have followed and are parked close by. He stops two feet before reaching the gate and raises his hands, indicating he's not armed. Men like this have a gun hidden on them at all times, and his men are packing for sure.

Guard doesn't drop his rifle, but rests it on his shoulder and steps forward. I'm one step behind him. With Ghost on the roof, he'll pick off anyone who tries to go for their gun. Risk and Saint are focused on the entourage.

"Well, gentlemen, it seems we have a situation," the older man says. Guard cocks his head to one side, his gaze piercing the man, but he remains silent. "My name is Aldo Capaldi. And you have something that belong to me."

"Never seen you before. Never done business with you, so I can't see how I have anything that belongs to you," Guard states.

"You have Rose Mariner under your roof." He nonchalantly flicks a hand at the building, his tone demeaning. Insinuating our home is not up to his standards. The pompous ass thinks we give a shit about his opinion.

"Rose is Thunder's woman. We don't sell women. We don't sell drugs, and we don't kill without reason. But give us cause and we'll burn you to the ground," Guard says menacingly, obviously taking exception to Aldo's derogatory comment.

"You can keep the girl. I have no use for her. I just want what's rightfully mine," Aldo replies.

"This is where we have a problem, because we have no idea what you're talking about," Guard says.

"Harvey stole from me. He died because of it. Unfortunately, he gave a very valuable gift to one of his whores. He didn't realize its value, or the rodent would never have given it away."

"And you think Rose has it?" I ask. "She's up to her ears in bank loans from starting her flower shop. If she had anything of value, she would have sold it."

"Her sister, Clarissa. I'm sure you remember her," he says snidely, "was seen with it. She's dead, but someone has my property. Clarissa had a fondness for her sister. I think she might have sent it to Rose. I only want what's rightfully mine." The way he talks, he knows about Clarissa's past. He knows she and I were a thing at one time.

"Rose and her sister weren't close. She didn't see Clarissa after she left their family and only found out about her death through the cops. No way does she have what you're looking for," I say.

"She has it. Various possessions were sent to her family. One of Harvey's girls saw him give it to her. It took her a while to tell me the truth, but she finally did." He pauses, then lowers his voice and in a sinister tone adds, "Right before she died."

He's talking about Cora. He beat the fuck out of the girl for information, then killed her when she had nothing more to tell. All this just to find out about this mysterious and valuable present that Rose may or may not have in her possession.

"You're talking in riddles. Either tell us what you're looking for and we'll see if Rose has it and have it returned to you, or this meeting is over," Guard pushes, taking a step forward.

The goon next to him reaches for his gun and aims the revolver at Guard. Suddenly, the whiz of a bullet hits the guy in the shoulder, forcing him to drop the gun.

"You shot my man!" Aldo exclaims angrily. "This was supposed to be a peaceful meeting." He glares at Guard, trying to intimidate him. That's useless on his part.

"Peaceful? Your idiot pointed a gun in my face, and you think my boys are going to let you play that way?" Guard growls. I can see his jaw clench. "Hear me and hear me good. Any other of your men get the idea to pull out a gun, it won't be a warning shot they get. It'll be a bullet through the heart." He gives Aldo a second to let that sink in. "And if you want something back that you think is yours, you gotta come clean with what you're looking for. No doubt in my mind that Rose has no clue. You're talking in circles and saying absolutely nothing that's getting either of us any closer to finishing this."

"A key. It's a fucking key," Aldo grinds out in frustration. It's killing him to have to divulge more than he's ready for.

"A key isn't a gift you give a girl. Why the hell would Clarissa even think it meant anything?" I ask.

"It's gold and fits a special safe. The only way in is with that key. I was told she had it on a chain, hanging around her neck," Aldo finally tells us. He's pissed he's had to tell us anything at all and is still leery, choosing his words carefully. Special safe? What the hell is that? Where is it? What the hell does this key look like? I have a feeling any questions I ask are going to be answered as vaguely as possible.

"We'll look for it. If we find it, it's yours," Guard declares. At this point, I couldn't give a shit what the key opens, as long as they leave Rose and her family alone.

"When you find it," Aldo insists, "either you hand over the key and I get what I'm looking for, or I come for your girl." He looks directly at me. I clench my fists, dying to reach between the iron bars of the fence and wrap my hands around his neck to squeeze the life out of him.

"Don't threaten Satan's Pride," Guard warns, his steely gaze locking Aldo in place. "No one touches Rose or any of the Pride. Do not make the mistake of underestimating our abilities. I'm going to allow this one verbal slipup to slide, but the next time, I'll cut your tongue out of your head and hand it to the idiot next to you."

"One week." Aldo takes a step back with an evil grin. "I'll be in touch." He turns to me. "There will be a day when you let your guard down, and I'll find a way to steal Rose right out from under your nose, *if* I don't get what I want."

They return to their vehicles and speed away from the club.

War breaks his silence. "What the fuck was that?"

"A desperate man who needs that key," Guard replies. I furrow my brow, not understanding his response. "That key belongs to his boss. Aldo Capaldi needs to get it back before the big man knows it's missing. He may be aware it's missing, and he's getting closer to finding out that Capaldi fucked up." Guard says this with such conviction that I know his sixth sense is kicking in. I have no doubt in my mind that he's right and this is going to get worse before it gets better.

"I'll talk to Rose," I say.

"Find out who has the last of Clarissa's effects. They ship it to the family, or it's given to them as soon as they release the body. A trip to Nebraska might be in order," Guard says.

"We can have Hawk approach Penny and Erik."

Guard shakes his head. "That's risky. The less they know, the better. We'll find a way to get you there under the radar. I'll see if Hawk can keep you under lock while you're in his territory, until you're ready to come back. But first, look through Rose's place to make sure it isn't among some of her belongings. Maybe her sister snuck it in and never told her."

"Unlikely, but you're right. We have to make sure," I say. "This meeting holds more questions than answers."

"We'll get there," Guard says with determination. I fucking hope he's right.

SEVENTEEN

Search and Retrieve

ROSE

I'm calm, thanks to Camille. When I look around the room, guilt mounts in my heart. The babies should be in their beds with their favorite blankies and stuffies. The moms should be nestled next to their husbands, enjoying their precious time alone. Because of me, actually, because of my selfish dead sister, we're locked away, in hiding.

Each time I think I'm over the anger, I'm forced to recall the ramifications of Clarissa's actions. It brings back all the memories of manipulation, sadness, and despair. The ache my mother felt when she knew Clarissa was lost to us forever, and the second-guessing of my parents' actions, wondering where they went wrong.

"I need to leave," I murmur, unknowingly aloud.

Camille pats my hand. "No, sweetie. You need to stay with us."

"I *have to* go. They won't stop until they get what they want, and I've put you all in danger. Kids shouldn't be subjected to this. *You,* all of you, shouldn't have to be tossed into a panic room."

"Thunder won't let you go," Camille reminds me.

"I need to protect him most of all." I begin to choke up once more. First, one Mariner sister puts him through hell, and now me. Granted, I didn't do this intentionally and I still don't know what all this is about or why they're after me, but it's very clear it's me they want.

VI must be listening, as she comes closer. "You told us you trusted us, remember?"

"Yeah."

"Do you still?"

I shake my head. "It's not about trust."

"It is. Do you trust us?" she asks again.

"Of course." My shoulders sag. "This isn't right." I wave my hand around the room. "You shouldn't be pulled into my sister's mess."

"Neither should a stalker have attacked me to get to Maddie. Neither should a husband beat the shit out of his wife, causing her to never be able to have babies of her own. Neither should a mother shoot her son's woman just for loving him as he should be loved. So much out there" —she flicks her hand to the steel door—"isn't right. Bad people exist. This isn't our first time in this room, and it won't be the last. Our kids are young, and they think this is an adventure. And when they get older, we're going to teach them what brotherhood and sisterhood is all about. Hell, we're doing that now." Vi takes my hand, squeezing it hard. "They've taken your sister from you and your family. Don't let them take Thunder away from you. Hold on with both hands. Think of the awesome reward you'll have when this is over," she says with a grin. "He's worth it, right?"

Before I can say a word, the door clicks and slides open. Guard and Thunder are front and center. As the ladies file out and into the arms of their men, Vi moves past Guard, and I hear her say, "She's a flight risk," half-teasing, half-serious.

"What happened to girl code?" I ask snottily, again partly kidding.

"Girl code goes right out the window when you're about to make a stupid decision," Vi retorts and walks into the arms of her husband.

My gaze moves to Thunder, who is eyeing me suspiciously. "Do I have to tie you to the bed?"

"You wouldn't dare!"

"I would and I will, but I was hoping to do that for other reasons and not because you're about to go from the frying pan into the fire," he says, standing with his legs slightly apart and hands on his hips. "Do you a solid, baby, when I tie you to my bed, let it be for the fun kind of reason," he rumbles in his sexy, smooth voice.

Guard has a sleeping Gavin in his arms, with Ava beside him with Ryder in hers as they walk past us. He stops to say, "Tomorrow, we're making plans. Those plans include *Nostra Casa*. Reno is going to know this guy. Get Rose caught up and get some sleep."

With Thunder and me the only ones left, I say, "Caught up?"

"We'll talk upstairs." He takes my hand and pulls me to my feet, then secures a solid arm around me.

"I won't disappear." I let out a heavy sigh. "I thought about it. I'm scared, but I'm more scared for you. If anything happens to you because of me—"

"It won't," he says firmly.

"How can you—"

"Because this guy is desperate and showed his hand tonight. This means we've got more to go on. We know what he's after, and we have a name." He turns to face me, dipping his head to kiss me softly. "This isn't about you. It's about a desperate man who's looking for a key that leads to some golden treasure, which he probably stole from his boss. We think the heat is on and he's trying to find a way out of the mess he got himself into. Clarissa just happened to be part of that plan, and now that she's gone, he doesn't know where to look."

I'm still highly confused, and it must be showing on my face.

"Let's get settled in bed, and I'll tell you everything. I'm not holding anything back. I wouldn't do that to you. We're a team, and partners say it like it is," he says. His words cause a warm, gushy feeling in my belly. I lean into him, banding my arms around his waist.

Looking up at his beautiful face, his gaze meeting mine, I say, "All right, partner. I'm all in. We'll see this through together." I hope I sound more confident than I feel.

"That's my Rosie." His lips touch mine.

Oh, that's nice. All of a sudden, I'm not so afraid.

Thunder told me everything that happened with this man, Aldo Capaldi. I've never heard of him and don't recall Clarissa ever mentioning his name. Then again, there's a lot about my sister I didn't know about. I lie awake for hours in bed, trying to think back on ever being given a key.

After Clarissa's death, the police gave us a bag with her clothes and what she had on her person when they found her. I don't remember seeing a key or any jewelry. Then again, who knows how long she'd been in that alley before her death was reported. If she had been wearing jewelry, any vagrant or thief could have taken it.

Eventually, sleep takes over. It helps that I was lying in my man's arms.

This morning, we're meeting with Guard, Ghost, and Orion in Guard's office. They're already waiting for us when we knock. I'm grateful for the pot of coffee waiting for us. I didn't get as much sleep as I would have liked and need the extra jolt of caffeine.

Pleasantries finished, Ghost is the first to bring up the topic of this mysterious missing gold key. "Any idea where Clarissa would have hidden it?" he asks.

I shake my head. "None. She sold anything of value for her next hit. I don't remember seeing anything like that. I recall being handed a clear plastic bag after she died. It had some ratty clothes, a small purse, empty except for a lipstick, and her shoes, but no rings or that sort of thing."

"Did she ever come home after she left?" Guard asks.

"No, not while I was there. I was taking courses in college and wasn't home twenty-four seven, but my parents would have said something if she ever did show up at the house."

"I'm not so sure about that, Rosie. Your parents might have been trying to shield you from that. Clarissa had a way of causing drama, even when she didn't mean to. You could hardly stay in the same room as her in the end," Thunder reminds me.

That is something my parents would do, just to keep the peace. I was tolerant of Clarissa's bullshit for a long time, but near the end, I couldn't keep quiet anymore.

"I did threaten to leave if they let her back in the house." I bite my lower lip, closing my eyes. "I made them choose between two daughters." An ache grows in my chest. "At the time, I was so angry that they would rush to her aid all the time, no matter how much crap she brought to our doorstep. I wanted it all to stop." I look up at the three men, then slide my eyes to Thunder. "I didn't consider how it would make Mom and Dad feel. I mean, how do you choose between your kids? I screwed up." Maybe it's the shitty sleep or the overwhelming realization that I had made it even more difficult for my parents, but a single tear runs down my cheek.

Thunder drags me from my chair and onto his lap. "Baby, you were dealing with an impossible situation. Your parents were struggling too. In the end, they took the hard stance and tough love approach. They'd already tried everything else. I know Penny and Erik pretty well, and regardless of what you said, they would have done what they thought was best for Clarissa."

Guard says, "I get that this is hard for you, Rose, but we need to go through your house and look for anything Clarissa may have given you."

"She never gave me a damn thing. She took and she took. She stole from me. I had to find hiding spots around the house where I could store my things. After my sixteenth birthday present went missing, I knew it was her, and I hid everything. Dad gave me pearl earrings, and a week later, they were gone."

"Let's check to be on the safe side," Thunder coaxes.

I shrug. "Fine."

"We're going to need to search through your parents' home too. If it's not with you, it might be with them," Ghost says.

"They moved. Wouldn't they have found it when they were packing?" I ask.

"Maybe, maybe not."

Guard says, "We don't want to bring Capaldi to your parents' doorstep. We have a plan to get you in and out of Nebraska. While you're there, we've asked Hawk and his men to step up and assist. They're all over it. Hawk's going to meet you at a private airport. He'll see you safely to the Mariner home and keep watch. Two days maximum, then I want you back."

"Hawk?" I ask.

"Yeah, babe. The guy looking out for your parents' safety." Thunder nudges my memory.

I nod. "Right."

"Reno is flying in his private plane. His pilot will take you and bring you back. Chances are we're being watched. We're going to use decoys to get you out. The flight plan will be altered once you land." Guard turns to Orion, who does a two-finger salute, saying he's on it. "Dante is gathering all he can on Aldo Capaldi. So far, we know he's a part of another Mafia family called *Ultimo Morte*. Reno is treading carefully on this one. Seems that he knows their leader and wants all the facts before having a face-to-face."

"When do we leave?" Thunder asks.

"Rose's place first. With any luck, we won't have to fly at all. If we find nothing, later tonight, you both fly out," Guard says. He nods to me. "How are you doing with this?"

"I'm good. The sooner this is over, the better."

"Mission: search and retrieve is underway," Orion jokes, lightening the mood, causing the men to chuckle. Even I manage a heartfelt grin.

EIGHTEEN

Aye, Aye, Captain

THUNDER

Luckily for me, Rosie is a stickler for keeping her place nice and tidy. Everything has its place. Only problem is, she still hasn't unpacked many of the boxes she brought when she came to town. This is both a blessing and a curse. We unpack every box and go through them with a fine-tooth comb, finding nothing that resembles a gold key.

Hours later and much more tired, Rosie plops onto her sofa.

"I knew it wouldn't be here." She shakes her head. "She's never given me a damn thing in my whole life. I can't imagine her giving up anything of value."

I hate to admit it, but I think she's right about that. "We're not done yet. Pack a bag, Rosie. We're going to Nebraska. I'll put these boxes back downstairs and call Guard."

"Mom and Dad are going to lose their minds when they find out what's happening," she says.

"We can make it a surprise trip home."

"I just opened the shop. They know I wouldn't leave."

"Willow and Charli are looking after the shop. You've got price lists tacked up on the board. The only thing they can't do is make elaborate bouquets. The situation may not be perfect, but your shop will stay open. You can tell your parents you have good friends helping you out for a couple of days."

"What if it's not there?"

"We'll deal with that when the time comes." I sit down next to her. She rests her head on my shoulder, defeated. "Erik and Penny knew who Clarissa was. We'll try to keep them out of it, but, if necessary, we'll fill them in and see if this magical key comes to light. I hate opening old wounds, but it might come to that."

"I hate this for them."

"Yeah."

I give her another minute, then urge her gently to go get ready. Risk is meeting us two streets over. Aldo's men have been watching the house, so leaving the same way we came isn't an option. War is out back and will guide us over to the car. "Demon and Sofia will be there shortly," Guard says over the phone. "Later, Saint and Abby will join them. They'll put everything away. It'll give them something to do while they hang out here. They're staying until late, making it look like you got people coming to help out. This will get you out of town and back unnoticed."

"Might work."

"It will. We'll have people moving around, coming and going. Two days is all you get, then you're home, with or without the key."

"Let's hope we find this thing," I huff, raking a hand through my hair.

"Either way, it won't matter. Reno's thinking this isn't

about money. He's been feeling out Raffaele, the big don of *Ultimo Morte*, and this guy, Raffaele, is a fucking beast. He's riled about something, but money doesn't seem to be his issue. This guy is all about loyalty."

"Can't we tell him about Aldo's visit?" I want this done and now.

"Reno's truce with this guy is new. He's feeling Raffaele out, and he's digging into this Aldo character in ways we can't. Hold tight, and by the time you're back, we'll decide how to move on this," Guard finishes.

A short time later, we're moving across the fenced backyard and out through an opening created by War, while Demon and Sofia are making themselves at home at Rose's place. Both War and I are on our guard, ensuring we aren't being followed to the airstrip.

As promised, a plane is waiting, and to my surprise, Sebastian is waiting for us. Sebastian is Reno's other brother. He and Dante are twins and look almost identical. He escorts us onto the plane and waits for us to settle into our seats.

"Good to see you, Thunder. It's been a while. Sorry it had to be under these circumstances," Sebastian says.

"We're getting the royal treatment if you're here," I jest.

"Yeah, well, they sent the best-looking bro," he quips. Sebastian has always been the more carefree jokester of the three brothers. He's also the most hotheaded, but he's just as ruthless as his siblings. Dante is known for his quiet, lethal nature and IT ingenuity. Reno is a man with vision. He's a strong leader and more dangerous than you can imagine.

It's fortunate for us that the bond between these men and Risk goes so deep that they would do anything for him. Risk took Dante and Sebastian in when Reno wasn't even aware of their existence. Risk raised them, looked after them, and found their brother, reuniting their family. For that alone, they will be eternally grateful.

That's not to say that Satan's Pride hasn't helped them out on an occasion or two. We've stepped in whenever asked, with the understanding that we never fall into their family business and they don't fall into the MC world.

"This is Rose." I turn to her. "This is Sebastian."

Sebastian extends a hand. "Good to meet you."

"Likewise. Thanks for doing this," she says quietly.

"Reno and Dante have filled me in. The plan is to get you in and out of Nebraska without anyone knowing. This guy Hawk will be waiting for you. I'll be back in forty-eight hours to come get you," he says.

"Appreciated. Let's hope we have better luck in Nebraska," I say.

"Reno and Dante are doing their thing. Trust, brother," Sebastian states with conviction. Glancing back to Rosie, he continues, "You don't know me yet, but suffice to say, you have the Pride and now you've got *Nostra Casa* behind you as well."

"Thank you, Sebastian. I just wanted this to be finished, and I don't want these people anywhere near my parents," Rosie says sadly.

"Ain't gonna happen, babe," I tell her.

The pilot comes out and tells us he's ready for takeoff. Sebastian takes his place opposite Rose and me. I'm glad Rosie falls asleep so that Sebastian and I can go over what we know about Aldo Capaldi and what more they've discovered.

"Aldo is an underboss for *Ultimo Morte*, with the smallest

territory and the biggest ego. He's had run-ins with the local gangs and started more wars than is necessary. At first, he and Raffaele got along, but lately, if rumors are true, not so much." Sebastian lifts his shoulders and throws out a hand. "But he has the position, and unless he does something extremely stupid, it's his to keep. Doesn't make sense that he's wasting time and manpower over a freaking gold key. There's more to it. We just haven't figured out what."

"He killed a woman for this key. He killed Harvey, her pimp, for this same key. It's got to mean something," I tell him, glancing over to check that Rose is still asleep. "Best-case scenario, we find this thing and give it back and we never hear from him again."

"Sure. But now he knows that you know it exists and that makes you a witness," Sebastian says.

"Aldo talked about this shit to the entire Satan's Pride clan. So what's he gonna do? Target us all?"

"Not if Reno has anything to say about it. We've got your back. I think the important thing to find out is why he wants it back so bad."

"Guard thinks he stole it and whoever he took it from is on the hunt."

Sebastian raises an eyebrow. "Interesting." A sly smirk crosses his face. "Maybe we can poke the bear a little and see what happens."

Now it's my turn to look confused.

"Raffaele has a tie with *La Famiglia*. We're all allies at the moment. Perhaps they had thoughts on how to bring up the topic."

"Don't put yourselves in danger," I tell him. Granted there's a pact between our brotherhoods, but that's not something I want strained.

"We're already in it. The minute he threated a Satan's

Pride, *Nostra Casa* was involved," he insists. "You know what Risk is to us. And we know what he means to Satan's Pride. As much as we want to separate ourselves, we're forever indebted to Risk."

Rose stirs beside me. I give Sebastian the sign that the conversation is over, at least for now. The rest of the flight is uneventful, and we finally land on a remote airstrip, where Hawk waits with a Ford Explorer and a half dozen of his men.

After a quick goodbye to Sebastian, we're moved from one mode of transportation to another. Hawk takes the wheel while I get in the passenger side, with Rose riding in back.

"It's been a while," Hawk says with a grin.

"Too long, man." I clamp a hand on his shoulder. "How've you been?"

"Living the dream. The club is growing. Got a couple of new prospects on board. The shop is making great money, the building rentals are doing great. Haven't got any complaints," he says. He looks in the rearview mirror, "I'm glad to meet ya, Rose."

"Likewise," she responds.

"We've been keeping close watch on your parents. Nothing out of the ordinary, except your mother sure has a thing for gardening," he kids.

"I'm a florist," she tells him.

Hawk lets out a roar of laughter. "A biker and a florist?" He shakes his head. "It figures. Apple doesn't fall far from the tree," he says. "You look a lot like your mom."

"That's what they say." She beams. "According to Dad, I have her determination."

"That's another word for sass," Hawk says.

"You hitting on my woman, brother?" I give him a look, all in fun, though. Hawk's a decent guy. And he's very popular with the ladies. Women would fawn over him, literally hang off him in hopes he'd take them home for the night. Yeah, he's that good-looking.

"Never. I know the bro code. Especially with you. We miss you out here. Sure you don't want to come back? We could use you." he says.

I laugh. "Laying it on a little thick."

He looks back at Rosie. "I can see why you won't leave. If I had a girl as pretty as that, I'd stick to her like glue too." Rose has a tinge of pink on her cheeks. "Shit! She blushes too." He's quiet for a minute, then asks, "How are you going to play this, anyway? Are you just going to knock on the door and say, 'Hey. We're home.'"

"That's the plan. I don't think they'll toss us out," I say.

"I'm safe," Rose says with a smile.

"See?" Hawk says. "Sass." He continues. "Got two men on the place day and night. If they see anything suspicious, I get a call immediately. The entire club rides out. It'll be easier on us if you can stay out of sight, but if you have to go out, give me a heads-up. You've got my number."

"The plan is to find this fucking key and head back," I tell him.

"I'll just tell Mom that I miss her cooking and we can be sure that we won't be going out," Rose says. Her mother loves her kitchen and feeding her family. She was always a fantastic cook.

"We're almost there. Do you want to let us out?" Rose asks.

"Sorry. Guard's orders. Right to the door," Hawk says.

"Not a problem. Erik and Penny know I run with the club. We'll tell them that the brothers wanted to help out in surprising them with our visit."

Rosie nearly jumps out of the car before the car comes to a full stop. I let out a warning growl, and she stops.

"Oops!" she cries.

"Rosie, wait for me to come to your door. We agreed that you stick by my side," I remind her.

"Aye, aye, Captain." She salutes.

NINETEEN

Family Reunion

THUNDER

Penny opens the door and yelps in delight when she sees Rosie standing on her front porch. She pulls her daughter in for a big hug as she calls out to her husband that they have company. When Penny finally releases Rosie so that her father can get in on the action, she takes me by the arm, seeing that my hands are carrying our overnight bags, and pulls me through the door.

"Drop those so I can get a proper hello," she says. I set down the bags and open my arms. Penny steps toward me, putting her arms around my waist and looking up at me. "We've missed you too, you know." I can see the emotion. Her face is soft, her eyes glistening. She's happy to see me.

"It's good to be back," I rumble, then drop my head to kiss her cheek.

"Michael," Erik calls to me, extending a hand. I take it, with one arm still around Penny. "This is a great surprise."

"We were hoping you'd think so," I say, shaking his hand.

We move through to their family room, where Rosie and her mom get to talking about her new shop. Rose pulls out her phone and begins scrolling through her pictures as they sit side by side, heads together.

"Let's get you a beer," Erik says. Which really means *I want to talk to you privately.*

Rosie's ears perk up. "Daddy—" she begins, eyeing her father warily.

"It's fine, babe. We're going to do our own brand of catching up," I tell her. I follow Erik out to the kitchen, where he pulls out a couple of beers, and then to the back deck, where we take a seat on handmade pine chairs. Erik likes to build, and this is part of his handiwork.

Erik takes a swig from the bottle. "You and Rose, huh?"

"Yeah."

"She's had a crush on you from the beginning. Never said it, but I could tell. Her mother could see it too."

"Rose was too young to get involved with someone like me. When I was with Clarissa, I was faithful, and I did all I could to make her happy."

"That relationship was chaotic. You were trying to save someone who didn't want to be saved." He sighs. "I could see the storm brewing. I knew it was only a matter of time before she pushed you away, like she did everyone else who loved her." He pauses and gazes into the sky. "Nothing I could have done to stop it."

"You tried." And he did. Erik did all he could to get help for Clarissa. Treatment centers, therapists, nothing stuck.

"We all did." He turns to me. "Where does Rose fit in?"

"The night I left, I wanted to forget everything and everyone. But the memory of Rose and her sweet nature would come to me time and time again," I tell him. "Never thought I'd see her again, so I carried on living my life.

Found a place that I made home with my club and the brothers. Dated and had fun. Then one day, I walk into a florist shop right in my town, and Rose come out from the back, and I'm stunned. I tried to ignore it, but I couldn't. Then she tells me she feels the same for me." I give him a moment to let it all sink in. "We talked about the past, and we've come to peace with it."

"She needs to be treated with care. Rose has lived most of her life overshadowed by her sister. That's another mistake I have to live with. Rose was always even-keeled, smart, and independent. I never had to worry about her. Clarissa was a mess and took up much of our time. Rose never complained. She just kept going on," Erik says, wistful and melancholy.

"Rosie's stronger than she looks."

"That she is, son. That she is," He takes another sip of beer. "Now tell me why you're really here." I'm about to tell him the story about missing her parents that we concocted before we left, but Erik raises his hand to shut me up. "No lies, Michael. I could always tell when you were covering for Clarissa."

I'm caught between wanting to keep him in the dark to keep him out of this disaster and giving it to him straight. He raises his brow, waiting.

"Clarissa's past has infested Rosie's present." This is going to be harder than I thought. Erik's face drops, the color draining from his face. "Me and my brothers have this under control. You've got to trust me."

"She's my baby girl," he whispers harshly, his expression pained.

"I've got men watching this house to make sure Penny and you are covered. Back home, I haven't left Rose's side since this started. The men in the club are stepping up, and we're going to get to the bottom of this."

"What do they want?" he exclaims. "Rose and Clarissa were never really close. Why go to her? Why not come to us?"

"You left and disappeared. My thought is that because she started her business, she was easier to find. The guy's name is Aldo, and he's looking for a key. Rose and I have checked her place from top to bottom. Nothing. Rose said her sister never gave her anything, but looked anyway. That's partly why we've come. And Rose really did miss you guys."

"What can I do?" he asks.

"Tomorrow, Rose and I have to continue our search. If you have anything that belonged to Clarissa or were given anything from her, we need to see it. Maybe a box arrived in the mail or something?"

Erik shakes his head. "I can't think of anything like that."

"We didn't want either of you upset. But it's your call whether you want Penny in on this or not."

"My wife is no dummy. She's probably grilling Rose for information right now. Rose wouldn't leave a brand-new shop, her dream, to come home for a visit. Chances are Penny's already got her spilling the beans."

"Probably."

"We might as well go in and face the music," he says with a wry grin. "In the morning, we'll all start looking."

"The hope is to find it. But just so you realize, the odds are against us. For all we know, Clarissa could have pawned the key for cash. Or it may have been stolen, seeing as she wasn't living in the best of neighborhoods."

He nods and gets up from his chair. I do the same and follow him inside. Erik wasn't wrong. We walk into Rosie telling her mother the entire situation, including her shop being trashed. She leaves out the part about the body being dumped. That would have thrown both her parents over the edge, and they're already freaked.

Penny's the type of woman who needs to keep her hands busy, so when Rose is finished, she goes back into her kitchen. While Erik is having time with his daughter, I decide I should try my hand at calming Penny down.

"You're banging those pots pretty hard," I kid. Penny looks over her shoulder and opens her mouth, but nothing comes out. She looks wrecked, tired and broken. I take a few steps closer and turn off the burner. I wrap a consoling arm around her shoulders and in a calming voice say, "I'm taking care of this."

"It's the mob, Michael. How can you take care of this?" She sounds despondent. "I've already lost one daughter. I can't lose another." She hiccups, tears on the verge of falling.

I hold her by her shoulders. "I love her. And I will not lose her. I know you don't know the men I call my brothers, but they're decent, solid men, and they don't back down when one of the family is being threatened. Rose is family, and so are you and Erik. This is the way we work. Our president, Guard, he's a force like no other. You need to believe me when I say we have the situation under control."

"What if the key isn't here?"

"We have a plan B."

Penny's lower lip trembles. "You need to look after my baby girl."

"Until my dying breath."

"You love her?"

"With all that I am."

She studies my face and releases a deep breath. Then she moves around me and turns the stove back on and stirs the ground beef. "I'm making spaghetti Bolognese. It was one of your favorites." That's the strength of the Mariner women. They suck it up and move on. I've seen it time and time again with Rose and Penny.

"Still is." I smile and get one back.

"Good. We'll enjoy a reunion dinner, then we'll get to searching," she says, regaining her composure.

Beauty and resilience, something both Penny and Rose have in common.

"Whatever you say," I tease.

TWENTY

This Can't Be It

ROSE

Thunder insists that we spend the evening together and reminisce as a family. He says, "Tomorrow will come soon enough. Tonight is about us." Dad agrees, and we talk into the evening about the shop, the club, and getting caught up on the family stuff my parents have been doing.

When it's time for bed, I expect Mom to put Thunder and me in separate rooms, but both our bags are in the bedroom the farthest away from them. Thunder takes it all in stride, whereas, I have to admit, I am a little taken aback.

My parents aren't prudes, but I thought that hearing about Thunder and me would take some getting used to. Apparently not!

Thunder gets ready for bed, stripping down to his boxers and sliding under the covers. I join him after my nightly ritual, and he drags me across to his side of the bed, tucking me in next to him. "Don't worry, babe," he says, "we're not doing the nasty." He snickers.

I playfully slap his shoulder. "Not funny. I was

wondering if they knew what they were doing when they put us together."

I can feel his body shake with laughter. "Your parents were our age once."

"Do not go there." I can't help emitting a gasp.

He laughs harder. "Sure, babe, but just saying, you had to get here some way."

I place my hands over my ears. "La la la la la."

Thunder rolls me onto my back and kisses me soundly on my mouth. "Good night, my Rosie," he says, turning off the bedside lamp and cuddling close.

The morning begins with Mom frying bacon and eggs while Thunder and I begin our search for the missing key. Thunder starts in the room we slept in, while I take the room across the hall where Mom had stored all our childhood mementos. The room is her craft and sewing room, but in the closet are a stack of boxes filled to the brim with things that belonged to Clarissa and me.

I'm saving them for last and decide to go through the drawers first. Thunder joins me soon enough. He pulls out all the boxes and takes everything out of the boxes, checking every envelope, every book, and every object. We're three boxes in when Mom calls us down for breakfast.

"It's getting cold." I can hear Mom's tone getting impatient.

I blow out a breath. "I don't want to stop."

"We won't take long. Come on, before she comes to give us hell." He takes my hand and leads me into the kitchen, where my parents are sitting and waiting for us.

I know my parents well, and when they exchange

glances at the table, it's obvious there's something on their minds.

"Spill, Dad." He looks at my mother, then lowers his eyes back to his plate, picking at his food, though he hasn't taken a bite yet. I look at Mom. "Mom?"

Dad clears his throat, then says, "We're thinking this thing that Clarissa was into was pretty bad. We're concerned this Aldo character isn't going to end it, even if he gets what he wants. What's to stop him from coming after you again and again?" He drops his fork, covering his face with his hands in despair. "Maybe we should get you out of the country. Help you to disappear for a while."

"No way!" I cry. "I'm not leaving everything I've worked for. I'm not leaving Thunder. Guard and the Pride have a plan. They've asked me to trust them, and I do." I grab Dad's hand and squeeze his fingers. "I'm not Clarissa. I'm not lost. I know who I am and what's important to me. You know me, Dad. I'm not going to spend my life running from this. I'll never have anything. I'll never be able to put down roots or have a family. I'll be looking over my shoulder and living in fear all my life."

"I don't know what to do," he whispers, his voice cracking with emotion.

"Help us," Thunder says. "Help us find this and try to remember as much as you can about Clarissa's last visit home or conversations. Did the police give you any of her things when they released her body to you? You may not think it's important, but it could be."

Penny lights up, her eyes growing wide. "Honey, the box. The box!" she exclaims. "Where is that box?"

Erik shakes his head. "What box? What are you talking about?"

"After the, huh…" Penny struggles with her words and manages an anguished "autopsy." Erik still seems confused, and Penny meets my gaze. "They had a clear plastic bag. I couldn't take it from the female officer. All I could see was her blood-stained clothes through the bag. The lady saw that I was upset, and she grabbed a brown box, put the bag in it, and taped the lid shut." She shakes her head. "I didn't even want to bring it home." She turns to her husband. "Do you remember that?"

Penny must have sparked a memory. He replies, "Yes, yes. I remember. You wanted me to throw it out as soon as we got home. I told you I couldn't do that. It was part of Clarissa, and I couldn't throw it away. It was like I was throwing her away."

"Do you remember where you put it?" Thunder asks.

"The garage, I think," he says uncertainly. "I debated whether to keep it or not when we moved here, but I'm sure I brought it with us. It's got to be in the garage. I didn't want Penny stumbling into it in the house and it upsetting her."

"Show me," Thunder says, rising from his chair. Both men disappear, leaving Mom and me at the table. I switch seats to sit next to her.

"It'll be all right, Mom," I murmur, putting my chin on her shoulder.

Thunder

Suffice to say, there's no way Penny would have found that box. It was buried deep in the rafters, behind a bunch of fishing equipment, covered with dust and still taped shut. It's wedged in tight between all the other stuff. I manage to wiggle it free where I can take hold of it easily.

I climb back down the ladder and set it on the workbench. "That's it," Erik confirms. "Never did open it. Couldn't bring myself to."

"I can do this alone." I can only imagine the pain of losing a child. This has got to be dredging up old wounds and hurt feelings. He's conflicted. His head wants to know if there are missing pieces to his daughter's death, and his heart has already mourned her death.

With a heaviness in his tone, he says, "I can't." He turns and walks back through the door to the house, leaving me to it.

I slice the tape with a box cutter in the toolbox and lift the lid. It's as Penny described: a plastic bag containing clothes spattered with Clarissa's blood. As I open the bag, a flood of memories of a young Clarissa with a vivacious laugh and a zest for excitement comes to mind. A senseless death due to drugs.

A short plaid skirt, worn and threadbare, a pink crop top, ripped in various spots, a pair of three-inch black stilettos, a small purse. No key. I try the purse. All I find are several condoms and a lipstick. I run my hands along the inside of the lining, but it seems smooth and untampered with.

Fuck! I was counting on it being here. No ID, no money, just a fucking lipstick. Clarissa's shade was hot pink. She had a thing for lipstick, and she had every shade of pink, but hot pink was her favorite. I hold it and take off the cap.

"Holy fuck!" I growl. No lipstick, but there is something lodged inside. I shuffle through the toolbox and find a pair of needle-nose pliers. It's a tight fit, but I manage to pull out the object.

It's the smallest gold key on a simple thin gold chain. "This can't be it," I say aloud, though there's nobody here to hear me. How the hell is this a key that leads to a fortune?

TWENTY-ONE

It's a Relief

THUNDER

I tuck the gold key and chain into my pocket. My gut prompts me to scan the items once again. I feel like I'm missing something. I run my hands over the material of the top, then the skirt. I hear a crinkle, like paper being crumpled.

There's something in the hem of the skirt. When I turn it inside out, I notice that parts of the hemline have been restitched. Carefully, I pull apart the thread to reveal folded bills of money. Clarissa was hiding money from her pimp, which is probably what got her killed. I pull out over a thousand dollars in cash with a note neatly folded, mixed in with the cash. "RD" is printed in capitals.

I fold and place the clothes back into the plastic bag as neatly as they were, then back into the box, firmly closing the lid before I climb back up the ladder to put it back where it was. Then I take out my phone and make my call.

Guard answers on the first ring. "Everything okay?"

"Yeah. You won't believe this."

"You found it," he says, and I can hear the sigh of relief in his tone.

"I got it," I confirm. "Something's not right, though. No way on this planet does this key open shit. It's a gold charm on a thin gold chain. It's not worth much of anything. You would get a couple hundred bucks at most for it, and that's being generous."

"Can't put a price on sentiment," Guard says. "Reno called Risk and wants to meet. I'm going with him. We're meeting at the cabin in the woods. Reno wants us out of sight and away from any ears. I think he's got the missing answers to this puzzle."

"Listen, I know we found what we wanted and could be on our way back tonight, but Erik and Penny are freaked. I couldn't keep them in the dark. I want to give them another night with Rose before coming back."

"That's fine. By that time, I'll have had the sit-down with Reno. I'll alert Hawk. He'll be there by noon to take you back to the plane," he says. "Stay alert."

"You got a feeling?"

"No, but we're close to the finish line, and I don't want to take any chances." He chuckles.

"The sooner this is over, the better."

After disconnecting, I slide my hand back into my pocket, tightening my fist around the charm. Hard to believe that this insignificant piece of jewelry has caused so many deaths and so much damage.

Erik is sitting in his armchair, staring out of the window deep in thought, when I come back into the house. I can hear Penny in the kitchen with Rosie. Erik must sense that I'm in the room because he turns to me with a pleading expression, silently asking me if I found what I was searching for.

I nod. His eyes turn to the heavens, offering a wordless thank-you. By this time, Penny and Rose have joined us, and I ask them to take a seat. I take my place beside Rose and tell them what I've found.

"A thousand dollars. Do—do you think she stole it?" Penny asks.

"I don't know. Rightfully, it belongs to you, but I'd like to hold on to it until this is sorted out," I tell her.

"Can I see the necklace?" she asks. I take it from my pocket and place it in her palm. "This isn't something she would buy for herself." Penny shows Erik, who takes it from her and studies it carefully.

"It's banged up pretty good," Erik says, turning it around in his palm. "Old." He's right about that. I noticed the same thing.

He gives it back to me, but Rose reaches to take it. "It's beautiful," she whispers. "A little piece of history. I wonder what stories this little key would tell if it could talk."

Rosie never ceases to amaze me. Where most see an old, worn-out, worthless charm, she sees beauty in everything. And she's right. It's priceless to someone. One being Aldo, who has killed two people to get to this key charm.

"I hope you don't mind if we stay the night. It'll be good to just sit and enjoy the company for a while," I say.

Erik and Penny seem happy about that. Rosie is ecstatic as she pressed her hands on my cheeks, pulling me down to kiss me soundly on the mouth. "You're the best!" she tells me.

I touch my forehead to hers. "I'll give you everything I have to give to see you this happy every day."

For the rest of the day and into the night, the problem looming over our heads disappears. I watch the interaction between Rosie and her family. The way Penny and

Rosie dance around each other, finishing each other's sentences while working to make dinner and bake dessert shows me all I've missed growing up.

I help Erik with the yard work, and after I moved some of the larger stones, I put away the mower, he's waiting for me on the deck with a cold beer and a pat on my back.

"Thanks, son. It's nice to have an extra hand. I've been meaning to move those stones. No way I would have been able to do it alone," he says. It hit me that he means what he says. "Penny calls her garden her oasis. She's going to be thrilled to see how neat and tidy it is, and now that those stones have been laid, she'll be able to walk through her flower bed easier."

It shouldn't be affecting me this much, a simple thank-you, but it does. This feeling of loss and missing out on what a family should be. This takes me back to being in our own yard, but instead of my father and me working together, it was me and the gardener he hired every season.

Clive was a nice older man with three kids of his own. The oldest was my age, and he came with his dad to help him out. Clive and Sam included me in their duo. Sometimes I would go along with them for the day. Clive told me to ask my parents. I never did, but told Clive I had. Funny thing is, I was gone all day and my parents didn't even know I was missing.

"Shake it off, son." I hear Erik's voice. Erik knows about my relationship, or lack thereof, with my parents. Back in the day, he asked about them, and my tactic was to either give bare minimum information or change the subject. Then one day, I got a call from Dad's PA requesting that I come home for an award presentation. Dad was receiving a plaque in his honor, and it would look good to have his son in attendance.

I was fuming. By the time I got off the phone, after

saying not-so-nice things to this poor woman who got the brunt of my wrath, I threw the phone across the yard and watched it smash into pieces when it hit the fence. Erik came out, didn't say a word, and waited, and then waited some more until I was ready. I gave it to him, the whole story. Along with the guilt of feeling the way I did.

In my mind, I wasn't beaten, I didn't have to scrounge for food, and I understood others did, yet I couldn't help what I felt.

"Neglect is as bad as a physical slap in the face. Actually, it may be worse," Erik told me. "Loving a child isn't about how much money you throw at them. It's about making memories that they'll hold on to even when we're not there."

And here he is again, watching me fall back down the rabbit hole and leading me back to the present. In true Erik form, he starts telling me about his last fishing trip with his brother and the family reunion they're planning in the fall. It was more of an expectation that Rose and I will find the time to be there so the rest of the family can meet me. Soon enough, the dark cloud overhead has blown away with the gentle breeze of the day.

Inside, Rosie and Penny are doing their own thing. They come out to join us. Penny sits by her husband; Rose is next to me. Rose slips her hand into mine, her face turned upward to the warm summer sun, basking in its goodness. All is calm.

The faint squeal of children laughing and splashing can be heard in the distance.

"Enjoy it, Michael. This is one of those moments," Erik says, shining a huge smile in my direction.

Rose

We're heading back home. I hate tearful goodbyes, and this time it was even harder. Dad was reluctant to let us leave, being a dad and all. He just wants to protect me and hide me away until this thing blows over. Mom was much the same, but she knows me well enough to understand I wasn't going to give up everything I've worked for without a fight.

Hawk is right on time, as is Sebastian. His plane is on the tarmac waiting for us.

"Thanks, brother. I owe you one," Thunder says, giving Hawk a manly hug.

"I'll remember that," he says with a grin. He grows serious, adding, "You know we're at your side, no matter when."

Sebastian welcomes us onboard and quickly says, "Change of plans. Guard and Reno are in New York. We're supposed to go direct."

"What's going on?" Thunder asks.

"You found the missing golden treasure," Sebastian says with a shit-eating grin.

I glance from one to the other. "What's happening?" Instinctively, I move closer to Thunder, who automatically tucks me into his side.

"I don't have all the details, but I got to say, you finding that key is a miracle," Sebastian says.

"Why New York?" Thunder asks.

"All I know is that Risk, Guard, and Demon are waiting for us for a private meeting with Raffaele Di Morte and his consigliere, Ivo. Reno and Guard want you to hand over what you found directly to the rightful owner." That's all Sebastian knows. He waits for us to buckle in before giving the go-ahead for takeoff.

Thunder can see my apprehension. "Guard wouldn't put us in a dangerous situation."

"Not intentionally," I whisper.

"There's history between *Nostra Casa* and Satan's Pride. The bond goes so deep that I would bet my life that Reno would never put Risk, Guard, or any of us in a dangerous situation. This is the end, baby."

"That would be a relief," I breathe. I dare to hope that this will soon be over.

TWENTY-TWO

It's Over, Baby

ROSE

I've never been to New York. The hustle and bustle of the city and the loud honking of irate commuters isn't something I would want to get used to. But the beauty of the architecture of the buildings and the grand theaters would be something I'd want to explore.

We seem to be traveling outside the city limits to an industrial area. It's another half hour before the limousine stops at a gated security fence. The guard moves closer as Sebastian rolls down his window, and he immediately opens up and allows us through. As we approach the warehouse, I become increasingly nervous.

This reminds me of a scene in a gangster movie. The kind where guns are drawn and, in the end, bodies are splayed on the ground, riddled with bullets. I look at Thunder, unable to hide my concern.

"I would die before I let them hurt you," he says as the car comes to a halt.

"I'd rather none of us die," I murmur. Guard and Risk are standing together with several other men. They all seem to be friendly, and Risk flicks his hand, gesturing for Thunder and me to join him.

"You ready, Rosie?"

"As ready as I'll ever be." I expel a heavy breath, taking Thunder's hand, feeling his encouraging grip as he guides me up the steps to meet the others. When Guard turns to face us, his expression gives away nothing.

We reach the top of the outdoor steps, on the platform where a pair of large bay doors are open. Inside, the place is stacked with crates nearly as high as the ceiling, and neat and organized. Nothing seems out of the ordinary, except it's Saturday and no one is here working.

"Gentlemen, this is Thunder and his woman, Rose," Guard nods toward us and continues with his introductions. "This is Nero, and his right hand, Luciano." Both men give a solid hello. "You've heard us talk about Reno," he says, pointing to the man on his left, then he indicates the man next to him. "And this is Dante, Reno's other brother."

Reno extends a hand. I place mine in his. He's being gentle and must sense my nervousness. "A pleasure, Rose. I'm sure this situation has been worrisome, but with any luck, this all ends today," he says with an encouraging smile. Reno is an extremely handsome man, with dark hair and dark eyes, a defined jawline, and perfectly groomed hair. He also seems very sincere.

"This business will be done," Dante says. He looks like a carbon copy of Sebastian, with the same blond hair and light eyes. If it weren't for their own distinctive style, you wouldn't be able to tell them apart. Where Sebastian is more outgoing and has more flair to his clothes, Dante seems more reserved and dresses in the same manner as his older brother, Reno.

"Thanks for stepping in and helping us out,"

Thunder says to Reno. He then turns to Nero and Luciano. "I want to thank you guys as well, for setting this up."

"We want to keep the peace and this truce in place. Seems to me that Rose here got roped into something she knows nothing about. We'll save the rest for when Raffaele arrives, but I'm certain he'll appreciate what we've discovered," Nero says. Nero is younger than the others, yet he seems wise.

"I'd just be happy to get this done," his friend says. Luciano is lighter in coloring, and you can see that these two men are inseparable.

As hot as all these men are, not one of them holds a candle to Thunder. It's not just that Thunder is exceptionally gorgeous, it's in the way he knows what I need before I do. He's protective, but in a way where I feel safe and I can still be who I am.

"Luce, you've always been the patient one," Nero ribs, playfully poking an elbow in Luciano's gut.

"Except I have a baby teething and Grazia is losing her mind," Luciano says, glancing at his watch.

Nero rolls his eyes. "Felicia and your mother are both with her." Luciano ignores his friend, takes out his phone and taps out a message. After an immediate bleep back, he relaxes when he glances at his screen.

"Finally, we can get this over with," Reno says. He raises his eyes at the Escalade coming through the gates and rolling to a stop beside the other parked vehicles.

I gasp at the height and breadth of the two men emerging from the car. They're massive! They look like heavyweight prize fighters who would not only beat you in the ring, but would do it just for shits and giggles.

"I think we're in trouble," I murmur.

"His bark is worse than his bite. That is, unless you

cross him, and then you're as good as dead," Sebastian says with a smirk.

"Jesus, Sebastian, shut it. Can't you see Rose is already freaked?" Reno gives him a stern look, then walks away from us and goes to greet our new guests. Reno and the beast exchange a few words, and when they come back, Reno says, "Let's take this inside."

Big badass MC and Mafia men can be gentlemen. They each step aside and allow Thunder to guide me into the warehouse and through the passageway first, into the office Nero points out to the right. The room is functional, with a basic wooden desk and shelves and not much else. They must have prepared for a sit-down, as the exact number of folding chairs are set up.

They wait for me to take a seat before taking one themselves. Reno is the first to speak. "This is Guard, the president of Satan's Pride MC, his men Risk and Demon, and this is Thunder and his old lady, Rose." He turns to Guard. "This is Raffaele Di Morte and his consigliere, Ivo." After a cordial handshake, Reno says, "There seems to be an issue that involves Rose and one of your men."

Raffaele quirks a brow. His penetrating gaze is set on me, scrutinizing me. "Go on," Raffaele says, his voice low and deep, almost a growl.

Thunder isn't happy, and I can see he's taken offense over the way Raffaele has started the discussion. This situation can get out of hand very quickly, so I decide to jump in.

"Huh, sir. This all started years ago with my sister, Clarissa. My sister had a drug problem and took off. She was an adult, and there was nothing my parents could do to convince her to come home. She was in too deep. We hoped that one day, she would come back on her own. Clarissa got involved with some pretty bad people." I pause as Raffaele tilts his head to one side with an expression that is saying, *What the hell does this have to do with me?*

"Then why is your sister not here instead of you?" he asks.

"Clarissa's dead. She was found in an alley. They attributed her death to an overdose. But the problems she was part of are overflowing into my life."

"How so?" Raffaele asks.

"A week ago, someone trashed my shop. We thought it was a bunch of kids, but when I got a call from some man who said, and I quote, 'I own you,' we figured it was more."

Thunder takes over for me. "When a dead girl was tossed out of a moving car directly in front of Rose's flower shop, we knew this was escalating. The only common factor was Rose."

"Then we received a visit from a man called Aldo Capaldi, who we now know is one of yours," Guard adds. Raffaele's ears perk up, and I can see that he's not pleased that he wasn't aware of Aldo's actions. "He works for you, yes?"

"He does," Raffaele confirms, those piercing eyes aimed right at me. "What is your business with Aldo?"

"None. He says I have something that belongs to him," I blurt out. "I had never met the man. He showed up at the club, and Thunder and Guard spoke to him."

"He came for a fight," Guard says. "And before you find out from someone else, we shot one of your men who pulled a gun in my house." Guard's face turns dark with fury. "No one comes to our club and makes demands."

"This is unfortunate," Raffaele concedes with a sigh. "I'll have a *talk* with Aldo." The way he says *talk* I think means he's going to beat the crap out of him.

"There's more," Reno says.

"Show him," Nero says, jerking his head at Thunder. "He needs to see it. Raffaele needs to know the extent of his man's deception."

Thunder looks first to Guard and waits for him to give him the go-ahead before standing and reaching into his pocket. He opens his palm to reveal the delicate chain with the gold key charm hanging from it. All eyes are on Raffaele. His jaw clenches, but his gaze never leaves Thunder's hand.

"This is the reason Aldo came after Rose," Thunder tells him. Slowly, very slowly, Raffaele tears his eyes from the necklace to look directly at Thunder. "He came to the club and threatened a war if a gold key wasn't returned to him. Rose didn't have a clue it even existed until Aldo said it was last seen with Clarissa."

I jump in to add, "My sister and I were never close. She would have been more likely to sell it for drugs. Thunder finally found it in my parents' garage in a box given to us by the police when they picked up Clarissa's belongings."

"Clarissa knew this was important." Thunder holds up the chain. "It was hidden in an old purse, in a lipstick case. I also found this." He shows him a wad of cash and the folded white slip of paper. He hands it to Raffaele.

Raffaele unfolds the notepaper and sees his initials.

"I don't know what this necklace means to you, and I don't need to know. All I want is for Aldo to leave us alone," I plead.

"May I?" Raffaele says to Thunder, indicating the jewelry. Thunder hands it to him. Raffaele raises it to his eyes, studying it, his fingers running over the gold key charm. "Aldo will be dealt with. You'll no longer be bothered." He then meets my gaze. "This was my mother's. A gift from my father. My father gave my mother many expensive trinkets, but this is the only thing she ever wore. When she was dying, she gave it to me and told me to make sure I held on to it until I found someone worthy of my love. I was married a short time ago, and this now belongs to my wife." He sighs and gives us a sly smile. "She deserves it for putting up with me."

Luciano was content to sit and watch as this all unfolded until this moment. "I understand this is your business, but I'd like to know how Aldo knew about the necklace and why he felt a dire need to kill to get it back."

"That's a very good question. I can only surmise that Aldo has something to do with its disappearance years ago. When it was lost, I was younger, and although it was bothersome, I had bigger issues to contend with. A short time ago, I went on the hunt to retrieve it. I've had my men scour every pawn shop and antique dealer. I found the right pawn shop, and he told me who bought it. I was tracking that man down," Raffaele says.

"That's why Harvey had to die. Aldo was afraid it would get traced back to him," Thunder says. "Then it just became a race of who would find the gold key first."

"He said the key opened a special safe," Guard says.

"I promised a safe containing a small treasure to the man who found my mother's gift. Aldo has been acting strange for months, and Harvey was one of his drug runners. This is all too much of a coincidence. My issues with my men are my concern, but rest assured, he will no longer be a problem for you."

Thunder moves to hand him the cash he still has in his fist. "This is yours."

Raffaele shakes his head. "It belongs to Rose and her family."

"No. It doesn't belong to us," I say.

"Then donate the money to a cause in your sister's

name," Raffaele says, then adds, "I do not condone killing innocent women, and I am truly sorry that this ugliness seeped into your life." He then turns to Reno and Nero. "Thank you for getting this back to me."

"It's all Reno who figured it out with his brothers," Nero replies with a chuckle. "Now you owe him twice."

"This one's a freebie, as long as Guard and his crew are left in peace," Reno says.

"You'll have nothing to fear from *Ultimo Morte*," Raffaele promises.

"Thank you, but Aldo may turn his attention to my parents out of revenge," I say, coming to stand before Raffaele. "I love my family, as you do yours. Please! I need your word."

"You have my word. I have never broken a vow, Rose, and I don't intend to start now," Raffaele says. Then he rises to his feet and bids goodbye to all, his friend Ivo following closely behind.

With everyone on their feet and satisfied that it's finally over, I say, "I can't thank you enough for all you've done."

Thunder hugs me tight to his side, his bright smile beaming down on me. "It's over, baby."

TWENTY-THREE

Choices

THUNDER

A *month later...*

Things go back to normal, or as normal as they can be seeing that Satan's Pride is never at a loss for excitement. Fortunately, the last bits of news include Abby and Ghost being pregnant with their first child. As always, the club rallied to celebrate the news.

To think that Ghost was a man without a name who remained that way for years and years before he made it home to his brother Guard is a miracle in itself. But that just proves how the love of a good woman can bring a man back to the land of the living.

Rosie has settled back into work. Her parents came to visit, needing to see for themselves that their daughter was safe. They stayed for the week, then made us promise to go back for the holidays before heading home.

"Take care of my girl," Erik said to me before boarding the plane.

"Always," I replied.

Erik and Penny are the parents I always wanted. They've suffered the loss of Clarissa, but they never stopped loving her. They encourage Rosie to follow her dreams and they pass no judgment on the Pride and how we run our lives. Erik was openly appreciative of the help Guard and my brothers jumped in to give. Penny told me I was a lucky man to have so many people who care for me. And then she made sure to say, "We do too." She came up on her tiptoes and kissed my cheek.

Rosie and I are unofficially living together. Either I'm in her bed in her home, or she's in mine at the club. With all that's happened, I'm letting Rosie set the pace, although I've already started looking for a house for us, where we can build a family of our own.

After Clarissa, and a string of other women who pretended to be something they weren't, I swore off women as a long-term plan. I rode free and wild and loved every second of it, convinced it was everything I wanted. Rose was an incredible surprise. A sweet girl, proud and strong, but also soft and caring, she's the whole package.

As I'm walking out to the parking lot of the compound, I see Guard dismounting from his motorcycle and coming toward me.

"Heading out?" Guard asks.

"I'm picking up Rose. We're meeting Saint and Izzy at Hanna's for a bite. Wanna come along?" I invite. He shakes his head, but he has a shit-eating grin on his face. "What's that for?"

"I told you, man," he says, and I know exactly what he's talking about.

When I made the decision to make the Pride my home, Guard and I had a heart-to-heart. It's something he does with all the brothers. Every man in the club has a special relationship with Guard. It's inexplicable, and each man keeps their conversation private.

I heard about this from the guys when I arrived. I was

preparing myself for a revelation, a significant life-altering, profound conversation. He took me out for a ride, two men and their bikes on the open road. We ended up outside town at a roadside diner. It was nothing to look at, but as soon as we walked in, an older woman greeted Guard like her long-lost son. Her nametag said Vera, but Guard called her Nancy. I quirked my brow, questioning this, but he ignored me and took a seat in the closest booth.

We each ordered a burger and fries, and then I sat back and waited for Guard to start whatever it was that he was going to say. For a long time, all he did was sit back and stare at me.

"What happens next?" I asked, extending my arms out. I couldn't stand the silence between us any longer.

"We eat," he replied.

"That's it?"

He slowly perused the diner, his gaze finally making its way back to me. "What do you see?" he asks.

"Huh?"

He repeated, "What do you see?"

I scanned the room. "Booths, people eating, food. What am I supposed to see?"

"You see what you see. It's not what you see, it's how you see it."

"I don't get it."

"Thunder, you're a wise man. You grew up way faster than you needed to, and you've lived. All the advice I would give a younger brother doesn't apply. Instead, I'm going to tell you what you already know in the hope that this makes an impact." Guard paused for effect before going on to say, "You're trying to lose yourself in the women you fuck. You've already figured out that it's fleeting gratification, a way for you to exhaust yourself so you can sleep. You dream about her. You think about her and your soul yearns for her. Do yourself a solid, go find her."

I knew he was talking about Rosie. The young woman who's haunted my dreams from the day I left after my rant on her family's doorstep. "Not meant to be," I responded.

"You can't escape destiny, brother. She'll find you."

That was it. The end of our talk. We ate. We left.

And here Guard stands, giving me that "I told you so" grin.

"Hanna, everything you make is so delicious," Izzy says before she takes another bite of her sandwich. It's got arugula, prosciutto, and provolone, with a vinaigrette dressing on a freshly made ciabatta bun.

"Baby, that sandwich isn't going anywhere," Saint chimes in with a laugh. "And you know you never finish it all."

I'd be surprised if Izzy could. That sandwich is bigger than her face. Izzy eyes her man suspiciously. "Watch me."

Rosie looks on, giggling, as Saint and Izzy banter. I just sit back in my chair and enjoy the calm of the day. Eventually, Izzy and Rosie move on to discussing the Lady Pride and their next get-together. This is when the men get anxious, because we never know the kind of trouble they're going to get into.

"We're not that bad," Izzy says when Saint rolls his eyes at the prospect of the women going dancing.

"Baby, when you women go out, we have to call in the reserves to make sure you all get home safe. Especially you, my delicious drunk," he teases, nuzzling into her neck. Izzy's cheeks go bright red.

"Jesus, Saint, take your woman home." This comes

from Risk, who enters through the back door that leads to Hanna and Risk's home. He comes in holding his son Romeo's hand. The backpack Romeo has strapped to him is bigger than he is, yet he's beaming with joy at seeing his uncles sitting at the table.

"Uncle Saint, Uncle T," Romeo exclaims, dropping his backpack on the floor and releasing his dad, then catapulting into Saint's waiting arms.

"If it isn't my little buddy. How was school today?" Saint asks.

"It was awesome. We played baseball, and I caught the ball three times." Romeo smiles happily.

"Do you have any hugs left for your Uncle T?" I kid, and as soon as I do, he slides off Saint's lap and runs over to me.

He wraps his arms around my neck and whispers in my ear, "Rose is really pretty. Are you going to marry her?" Romeo thinks he's being quiet, but Rosie hears him and lowers her eyes and stares down at her plate.

"That's my plan. Think you can talk me up? Make me look good?" Romeo's laugh makes his belly jiggle.

"It's gonna take more than that," Saint jokes.

"I hate to spoil the fun, but I need a word with Thunder," Risk says. He looks at his son. "Do you think you can keep these three out of trouble until I get back?"

"I'll keep an eye on them," Romeo says, puffing out his chest. The kid's going to be a loyal Satan's Pride brother when he grows up. I sit him in my chair and watch as Rose breaks her brownie and gives half to Romeo. He snuggles closer to Rosie and goes on chatting about his day.

I follow Risk outside. He leans his back against the brick and says, "Aldo Capaldi's dead."

"Say what?"

"You heard me. I got the call right before I picked up Romeo. Reno called and gave me the news."

"Aldo stole the charm. But why? The thing was virtually worthless."

"Raffaele's not talking. He told Reno to send word that we'd never have to worry about Aldo again and said he's been dealt with, permanently," Risk tells me with a heavy sigh. "I can only guess, but it sounds like Aldo took it years ago out of spite. When Raffaele went looking for it, Aldo panicked and tried to return it. It appears Harvey may have helped himself to it, and the nightmare progressed. From what I'm told, Raffaele's a private man, and his relationship with his family was complicated. He alluded to the importance of that gold key at the meeting. Will we ever know the details? Probably not."

"I don't give a shit, as long as they leave us alone." I'm fucking glad it's over and Rosie and the Pride are safe.

"Your choice if you want to share with Rose." I furrow my brow in confusion. He says, "Things have been good. Why dredge up the past? It'll bring back the pain of her sister's death and two others."

"I don't like to hide shit from her."

"Then don't." He shrugs. "You know her better than anyone." He pauses. "Maybe give her the choice."

"Yeah, maybe." I mull it over, and the more I think on it, the more I like the idea of giving her the choice.

TWENTY-FOUR

Home is Rose

ROSE

"I don't want to know," I tell Thunder firmly.

"Babe, are you sure?" His face is filled with concern. "Closure and all that. I don't want you ever thinking you have to look over your shoulder."

"Just tell me it's really over. I trust you to tell me the truth. I can move past this if you tell me I can."

"It's over," he says with finality. I breathe a heavy sigh of relief. We walked away that day from the warehouse shell-shocked. Eventually, I began to believe the promise Raffaele Di Morte made. Up until this moment, I'd put Aldo Capaldi out of my head.

"Good." I nod and plop onto the sofa. Thunder sits with me, his feet propped on my coffee table and his arm on the back of the sofa. Thunder lays his head back, and I get a good look at his face, beautiful, but tired. He's lost sleep for me. Even now, his worry was about my reaction. Yet Thunder ensures that I make the decision when I know he would have preferred to keep this stress from me.

The tight V-neck T-shirt displays the muscular column

of his throat and fits his torso, showing off his six-pack. Even his thick thighs and feet seem sexy to me. I'm not usually the one who initiates sex, but Thunder is irresistible.

I swing my leg over, settling on his lap with my legs on either side of his, straddling him. His eyes blink open, but before he can say a word, I press my lips to his neck, then let my tongue trail to his ear, where I nip at his lobe.

"Rosie." His voice is hoarse with need.

"Yes, baby," I murmur, my hands trailing down over his chest and under his tee. His warm, smooth skin under my touch spurs me on, and the moan of delight from his lips gives me excited butterflies in my belly. I raise his shirt, and he finishes the job, tugging it over his head and tossing it behind him.

His hands come to my thighs, slip under my skirt, and pull it up to my waist. He presses my lower half into his, moving me over him, rocking over his cock. With every movement, I get wetter and wetter. My fingers glide over his belt, undoing it quickly and unzipping him. I wrap my hand around his cock, firm and hard, yet soft and smooth.

Thunder returns the favor, unbuttoning my blouse and gliding it over my shoulders and down my arms, causing a tingle along my spine. My bra follows immediately after.

"You're the most beautiful woman I've ever seen," he says, then cups the back of my head and smothers his mouth to mine in a kiss that transcends any other we've had. This kiss is a promise of forever. It's unity, joy, completion, exaltation, yet calm, real, true, and free. How one kiss can say all that we are when we're together, I have no idea, and I don't care as long as I get to have this every day of my life.

"I want to take care of you," I say when our lips part. Thunder doesn't say a word, but motions for me to move off him. He pushes the table back with his legs, then plants his feet on the floor as I stand before him. He splays his legs and tosses several throw pillows down and waits for me to make my next move.

I drop to my knees on the soft pillows, my fingers tracing a path along the inside of his thighs and around to his hips, hooking my fingers into his jeans and yanking, although they wouldn't budge if Thunder didn't accommodate my request, shifting his weight, and I pull them off, exposing his swollen cock.

I lick my lips, my eyes fixed on his.

"With you on your knees, just like that, I may blow with your mouth on me," he says, his tone rough and needy.

"We can't have that. I want to taste you." Placing my lips over the tip of his cock, I slide my tongue through his slit. A hint of salty and manly goodness has me taking more of him. He's a big man, all of him. It's impossible to take it all, but with every little bit more, a groan of desire from my man surges through my pulsating core.

His fingers rake through my hair, lifting it off my face. Our eyes never waver from one another's. My mouth feels the throbbing of his cock. Thunder tugs on my head as a warning, but I stay fast to my task, wanting to swallow him down. An amazing spectacle unfolds in front of me when Thunder roars his release. His eyes close for a split second, but then his gaze holds mine, his expression sated and warm.

Thunder drags me upward, then turns us so I'm lying beneath him on the sofa. He presses himself into me and buries his face in my neck. "In ten or twenty minutes, I'm going to return the favor, then I'm going to spend the rest of the night showing you how much I love you."

Thunder did just that until the early morning, when we finally fell asleep in each other's arms, only to be awoken by the incessant ringing of his cell phone.

"Shit!" I hear from my man. I turn on the bedside lamp to see him staring at the phone screen.

"Who is it?" I mumble, unable to keep the sleepiness out of my voice.

"My mother," he grumbles.

Well, damn! This is a first! Not only does Thunder rarely speak of his family, never in all the time I've known him has he spoken to his parents in my presence.

The ringing stops, with Thunder still looking down at his phone, only to start again seconds later.

"Are you going to answer, baby?" I urge gently. His finger hits the green button, and he grumbles a simple "Hello" into the phone.

I can't make out what's being said, but the high-pitched frantic sounds of a woman on the other end are going on and on in Thunder's ear. He lets her rant, offering an occasional "Uh-huh," "Got it," and ends with "See you soon."

He grips the phone with his fist so hard, I'm surprised it doesn't crumble. Thunder looks at me and says, "I gotta go back. My father had a heart attack last night. He didn't make it. My mother wants me home for the funeral." He doesn't sound sad or broken. He sounds cold and empty.

I lean into him, my head on his shoulder. He tilts his head to that side, pressing it to my temple. "I'm sorry, baby."

"Nothing to be sorry about. I hardly knew the man," he says. His words may sound cold, but I know he's hurting.

"I'll start packing," I murmur. As I begin to move away, he pulls me back, hugging me close. This is his way of grieving. No words, but needing to feel me close. I give him what he needs and wait for him to let me go.

As I pack, he calls Guard to advise him of the situation and to let him know we'll be gone for a few days. "I'm going for the funeral, then home," he says matter-of-factly. I'm not sure what Guard is saying on the other end, but Thunder concedes when I hear him say, "Fine. We'll wait for Hammer." He pauses to listen once more before thanking him and hanging up. Thunder turns to me. "Hammer's coming. Orion's booking tickets for the early morning flight at six."

He sounds funny, and I don't know what to do for him, so I do the only thing I know how. I go to him, sit on his lap, and love him. I hold on tight, his arms flexing around my waist, and there it comes, the wave of pent-up anger and sadness rolling into an explosion of tears from my giant of a man.

Guard

I stare down from the top of the hill at the funeral going on below for Aaron Roger Donally. Thunder stands next to his mother in a tailored black suit and dark sunglasses, her arm through his on one side and Rose on his other side, their hands entwined. Hammer is next to Rose, keeping a close eye on his brother.

There are a lot of people, but from what Hammer told me on our last call, Thunder doesn't know any of them. His mother didn't call him for comfort, but because it wouldn't look good if their only son and child wasn't present at his father's funeral. Thunder gave his mother what she wanted, as he's done for all of us.

Thunder does that for the people he loves, whether they love him back or not. He's set his boundaries with his parents, but that doesn't mean he doesn't feel for them. That separation is self-preservation.

Ava takes my hand as she stands by my side. My woman understands what the Pride truly means. Not just about the club, but the tie that binds us. Thunder must be sensing our presence and his gaze finds us on the hill. We're all there: Orion and Vi, War and Maddie, Risk and Hanna, Saint and Izzy, Ghost and Abby, Demon and Sofia, Steady and Camille, Priest and Quinn, leaving behind Wildcard and Charli with Roscoe and Willow to look after our kids.

I put my hand on my heart, and the others follow suit. Thunder responds with the same motion. He knows that family isn't those who gave you life, but those who fill your life with joy.

A *week later…*

With the barbecue in full swing, it's my and Thunder's turn at the grill to give Rose and Saint a break.

"How are you doing?" I ask.

"I'm good," he replies, facing me. "Really."

"Your mother?"

"She's moved on. Her world continues without my father. She has her routine, her friends. She doesn't even know I'm not there."

"I guess it's true what they say for some: you can't go home."

"I am home. Home is this. Home is Rose." Thunder glances to where Rose is sitting with some of the other women, laughing loudly. Her head is thrown back, her hair in a tight ponytail. She notices Thunder and blows him a kiss. Thunder repeats, "Rose is home."

TWENTY-FIVE

Who the Hell Is She?

HAMMER

That's the biggest moving truck I've ever seen come to town. The old Bell Blue cottage, as it's called, has been completely renovated. I know this because Risk was the contractor for the job. It's far from a cottage. It's a two-level, three-bedroom home with a solarium especially added on by the new owner. A high-end reno, according to Risk. The owner spared no expense in getting what they wanted and never once squawked about the cost. Risk says Francesca Deleigh was the easiest client he ever had to work with.

I'm not a snoop, but it's hard to ignore since the back of the compound aligns with the road to the only house within walking distance, and that house happens to be Bell Blue cottage. When a bright blue Mazda CX-50 drives into the lane and parks next to the moving truck, I'm curious to see the new owners.

"Getting a glimpse of the rich and famous?" Risk teases. His lips form a sly grin.

"To be honest, yeah."

A woman exits the driver-side door, and even if I can't see her up close, I know she's a looker. A long blonde mass of waves cascades down her back, a headband keeping it off her face. She's toned and fit. Not a skinny nothing, but a woman who takes care of her body.

What's noteworthy is that no one else exits the car. "Where's her family?" I ask. There's something about her movements. The way she reaches out to touch the newly painted railing on her porch, the way her eyes follow the birds in flight, and how she drops her bag next to the rocking chair and takes a seat, like this is where she's meant to be.

"No family. Just her."

"Who the hell is she?" I ask, not expecting an answer.

"Just a woman," Risk replies.

No way in hell is Francesca Deleigh "just a woman." This I know because I've seen and been with plenty of women, but never have I felt so compelled to get to know all there is to know about any of them like I do about this one.

Risk walks away, leaving me to enjoy the view of a simple woman rocking on her porch.

Songs and Artists

"Chemical," Post Malone

"Eyes Closed," Ed Sheeran

"Die for You," The Weeknd

"Jaded," Miley Cyrus

"Trustfall," P!NK

"What a Night," Flo Rida

"Summer Baby," Jonas Brothers

"Never Ending Song," Conan Gray

"Landslide," Dixie Chicks
"I Don't Want to Miss a Thing," Aerosmith
"Breathe," Faith Hill
"One Thing at a Time," Morgan Wallen
"Look What God Gave Her," Thomas Rhett
"Pretty Lady," Lighthouse

Thank You

Thank you for Reading Thunder's story! Thunder and Rose are the couple that was never meant to be until one day, there she is and he can't deny his feelings any longer. Thunder dated the wrong sister but by the time he figured it out, it was too late, or was it? Next up is Hammer! Hammer comes from the army life, and he thrives on the brotherhood of the Pride. One look at the new girl in town and he knows he's got to get to know her. Hammer never has trouble with the ladies, except Francesca doesn't seem to be interested in the least. The Satan's Pride series continues with a new couple and their incredible journey and a new threat that emerges trying to keep them apart. Please look for Hammer, coming soon!

About the Author

AG Kirkham

I was born in a small town in Italy. My parents are loving people; and true traditionalists. I grew up being a chatterbox of a child and evolved into a quiet and shy teenager. I was definitely not the life of the party. As a matter of fact, I never wanted to go to any high school dances or any activities the school offered. I was good with being alone. I had to grow into my own and I eventually became the fun loving, open-minded and creative person I am now. I love the 'me' I have become and I am grateful that this is where I have landed.

Writing is my release and I have escaped in my imagination to some incredible places meeting the most awesome characters. I also wanted to be a rock star but anyone who has ever heard me sing kindly convinced me that I do not have any talent. (In other words, I suck at it.)

Although I have been writing since I was in grade school, and I am a hopeless romantic.

Reign of Pride is the first book in the Dark Reign series. I am currently working on the next in the series as well as continuing with my Satan's Pride MC Series. Each book introduces characters who you will learn about in the next series.

And lastly, I love to travel. I want to enjoy all that life has to offer. I want to meet people, learn from them and create the most fantastic, sexy love stories. If I can do this overlooking the ocean and feeling the breeze wash over me then I have my heaven on earth.

Stay tuned for more novels in the Dark Reign and Satan's Pride Motorcycle club series coming soon.

To stay up to date on all my book news please sign up for my newsletter HERE and follow me! All my social media links are below!

Also by A.G. Kirkham

Biker Romance

GUARD

WAR

ORION

RISK

DEMON

SAINT

CRIS

GHOST

ROSCOE

WILDCARD

PRIEST

Dark Reign Series (Mafia Romance)

Reign of Pride

Reign of Temptation

Reign of Possession

Reign of Turbulence

Reign of Rapture

Reign of Desire

Reign of Destiny

Reign of Loyalty

Reign of Compassion

Hidden In Plain Sight Series

The Sting

Innocent Bystander

Shots Fired

Acknowledgments

When the girl of your dreams comes waltzing back into your life, you seize the moment. Thunder was dating the wrong sister all those years and when the relationship went from bad to worse, Thunder cut his losses and left. He never thought he'd see Rose again but when he does, he's not going to let this opportunity pass him by.

Once again, to my loving family (Rick, Giulia, Antonio, Daniel, Samantha, Luca, Lia and Mila and Alessio) thank you for always believing in me; to those closest to me (you all know who you are), you give me hope and clarity, you mean the world to me. I would not have had the courage to take this voyage without you all. You have all been my inspiration and whose consistent support and optimism helped make this dream come true.

Thank you, Julie and Linda, for the beautiful book jacket and impressive work, as always. Your hard work and extreme patience are greatly appreciated.

Laurie, every day on this journey with you is brilliant. Working with you has been amazing and I value the friendship that has resurrected from this time together. To all of you that that jumped in and assisted me in seeing this book through until it was perfect, I want to sincerely tell you how much you are appreciated.

Printed in Great Britain
by Amazon